Amélie Rives

**Barbara Dering**

Vol. II

Amélie Rives

**Barbara Dering**
*Vol. II*

ISBN/EAN: 9783337038779

Printed in Europe, USA, Canada, Australia, Japan

Cover: Foto ©Andreas Hilbeck / pixelio.de

More available books at **www.hansebooks.com**

# BARBARA DERING

BY

## AMÉLIE RIVES

AUTHOR OF 'THE QUICK OR THE DEAD?' ETC.

'——— Life teaches us
To be less strict with others and ourselves :
Thou'lt learn the lesson, too. So wonderful
Is human nature, and its varied ties
Are so involved and complicate, that none
May hope to keep his inmost spirit calm
And walk without perplexity through life.'
GOETHE : *Iphigenia*

IN TWO VOLUMES

VOL. II.

London
CHATTO & WINDUS, PICCADILLY
1892

## XXII.

BRANSBY had never before been called upon to face such a problem as that which now presented itself. After a night and day spent in uncomfortable consideration of the matter from every aspect, he was forced to admit that the time had come when his wife could no longer be coerced by a disapproving word or glance, and that she was fully determined to carry out her intention of thinking and acting for herself. As for Barbara, her influence in all this was very apparent. That it was an unconscious influence Bransby did not know, and certainly could not have been expected to imagine. He regarded her as one of those alluded to by St. Paul, 'who creep into houses and lead captive silly women,' and his feeling of animosity to her was not decreased by his realization of the justice of many of his wife's personal remarks.

Altogether, Barbara stirred in him sentiments of a nature akin to those which the heirs of a blind person would probably feel towards a physician who had restored him to sight when his former state of darkness would have better suited their interests. To the weak no sensation is so delightful as that of power, whether worthy or unworthy. A vague suspicion of his own lack in certain virile qualities had been lulled, for Bransby, through all his married life, by the unquestioning sway which Eunice had allowed him to exercise over her.

It pleased him to see this bright young creature become staid, meek, reserved, at his behest, to hide the beauty of her arms and throat from others because he desired it, to lock up her favourite music and refrain from singing all but sacred songs because he found this course preferable. He had restricted her reading, dictated her occupations, overlooked her correspondence, and even selected her hours for exercise. He had occasioned her much suffering during the illness of her children, because, as a devout Tolstoian, he did not believe in doctors, and would never send for one until the last moment.

In all this petty indulgence of an egoistic authority he had found that curious delight which some children find in pretending that their image in the glass is a real person, although they know perfectly well that there is nothing substantial behind the frame. It was in his character as reflected in Eunice's submission that Bransby found compensation for the emptiness which existed in its actual counterpart. There was a tinge of the bully in his composition, if so masculine a word can be used in so shadowy a connection, and now that his victim, his 'fag,' as it were, had turned and faced him the idea of attempting to reconquer his old position never occurred to him. His chief thought was how to acquiesce with the greatest show of firmness and dignity, how to agree to his wife's requests without seeming to have been forced into an agreement; in a word, how to assume the attitude of one who bestows a benefit, rather than of one who accedes to a demand. Above all, he was almost feverishly anxious that his sister should not know what had taken place.

To Eunice, however, the hours of waiting were almost intolerable. She knew him thoroughly in most respects, but this situation was so unlike any in which they had ever been placed before, that she could not depend on her past knowledge of his character to decide upon the position which he would now take. She even thought that he might make a desperate resistance and come to some extreme resolve, such as a sudden sale of The Poplars, for instance, or a threat to intercept Barbara's letters. Many wild conjectures passed through her mind during the night and day that followed his visit to her room.

She was, therefore, entirely unprepared for his calm and amiable manner the next evening, when, following her into the library after dinner, he placed himself, with sedate deliberation, between the arms of a fragrant leather chair. He looked at her, smiled, softly tapped his finger-tips together.

' Well, my dear, have you quite recovered from your nervous attack of last night?' he asked suavely.

'You still look pale, I am sorry to see, but those blue shadows under your eyes have gone. It is not so damp to-day. That is always better for your neuralgia.'

'Oh yes, the weather is much softer. The roses have opened on several bushes to-day. This knot I have on, I cut it near the door.'

'Those pale flowers always suit you admirably,' replied Bransby. 'You have no gown I like better than that deep-green velvet, and the little Venetian ruff suits the contour of your face.'

'Yes, it is very pretty, and so warm. But my velvet is getting shabby, I'm afraid. Do you want me to get another green one, or would you rather have a different colour?'

This appeal to his taste and authority fell soothingly upon Bransby's disturbed self-confidence. He replied graciously that he could think of nothing more charming than an exact reproduction of her present costume, adding, in a by-the-way tone:

'Er—those matters we were speaking of. I wish to explain to you that you have indeed mistaken me, if you think I want you to educate our daughters according to my sister's ideas. That I consider many of her ideas excellent I must admit, but I also think that the mother is the only proper guide for her children.'

'I am very, very glad that you agree with me,' said Eunice, in a low voice. Her heart was beating fast, but her delicate face and figure wore their usual composure.

'And—er—I have also decided, after long and serious thought, that I do not wish to interfere with your friendship for Mrs. Dering; that is—er—in reason. I am willing to admit that her unfeminine views and decided manner of expressing herself may have prejudiced me against her. Indeed, she must have some good qualities to have won your affection, my dear.'

And here he bent upon her a benign smile. Eunice was too amazed at the completeness and ease of her victory to speak for some moments, not allowing for this parrot-like quality of succumbing at once to firm handling.

'It is very good of you to admit so much, Godfrey,' she said finally. 'I hope that you will know Barbara for yourself some day. But until then I don't want to have her here against your wishes. Apart from annoying you, it would be very unfair to her——'

'Oh, I can trust to you to keep things within bounds,' said Bransby blandly. 'Besides, she does not like me any better than I like her, I fancy. She generally goes straight to your room when she comes. There is one little matter, however, in which I hope you will oblige me. I heard Winifred attempting to whistle the other day, and when I reproved her she said, " Mrs. Dering does it." Now, I may be old-fashioned, but I do most certainly object to a woman's whistling. I hope you will make Winifred understand this.'

'Yes — yes, indeed, Godfrey !' exclaimed Eunice, with a touch of eagerness. She held out her pretty hand, crusted with darkly-glowing jewels. 'You may depend on me not to teach them anything of which you actually disapprove ; only in matters of a more personal nature I feel that I alone must judge for them. There are some things that a father can never under-stand——'

'Oh, certainly, certainly,' assented Bransby, also

with an approach to eagerness. 'I understand that entirely.'

His relief at having accomplished what he wished, and actually having her treat him as though he had conferred a favour upon her, so pleased him that he not only took her extended hand in both his own, but ended by placing his moustache carefully upon its satiny back before releasing it.

'As to some of the other things to which you alluded,' he went on, in the same easy tone, 'I cannot help thinking that you were overstrained, my dear. I know how delicate your nervous system is—how it responds to the slightest friction—and I can also understand how, at times, Lydia should annoy you, although with the best intentions, for I do not think her in the least hypocritical. But, as I was saying—forgive me, my dear, if I tell you that I do not think you are capable of judging—I have always guarded you as carefully as a florist some rare orchid. You do not dream of the brutish natures of most men. My extreme consideration may have seemed to you coldness, but I am persuaded that, had you been married to an ordinary man, you would have died of horror within a year.  These matters, however, are not for tenderly-cherished women like yourself to discuss.  You cannot, in the nature of events, know anything about them. Brutality, sensuality — what are they but names to you?  Only I beg that, before you condemn me as cold and unfeeling, you will also try to realize that self-control, consideration, restraint, are the highest proofs of respectful devotion which any man can show to any woman.'

'You are very kind—very, very kind to me, Godfrey,' said Eunice, with that increase of adjectives which so often denotes lack of spontaneousness.  Bransby was deeply content.  He felt that his chaste bit of oratory had accomplished even more than he had hoped.

In this second interview Eunice's tact had served her as good a purpose as her firmness during the first, and if she had dragged her husband protesting from his perch of self-esteem, she had certainly succeeded in stroking to a dandy-like gloss his ruffled plumage.

Before going to bed Bransby also had a conversation

with Mrs. Crosdill regarding her general attitude towards Eunice and the children.

'You know, my dear Lydia, how sympathetic your views are to me, but Eunice is a very high-strung woman. We must make allowances. Allowance should be made for natures not naturally religious and well-balanced like our own. You remember what the Apostle says: "To the weak became I as weak that I might obtain the weak."'

'Yes, but he never said that to the blasphemous he became blasphemous, or to the headstrong headstrong,' retorted his sister sharply.

'He said that he became all things to all men,' ventured Bransby somewhat timidly.

Mrs. Crosdill frowned over the elaborate altar-cloth which she was embroidering in gold bullion on a crimson velvet ground. Her next sentences were punctuated by sharp jerks at the needle, which seemed to relieve her feelings in somewhat the same manner that a series of silent oaths might have done.

'My dear Godfrey, I have always been convinced that the verse which you quote was improperly translated in the first instance, or more likely taken down incorrectly by St. Paul's amanuensis. You will remember that he often dictated his epistles. Bishop Cammersell told me only last month that such mistakes must frequently have occurred.'

'Of course. I am sure of it,' Bransby hastened to admit. 'But, at least, we know some things which are beyond dispute. "And if meat cause my brother to offend." There can be no discussion about that, I suppose. That is what I wish to call your attention to in regard to Eunice. She is a devoted mother.'

'Say rather a foolishly indulgent one, my dear Godfrey. I have never known a child who gave way to such paroxysms of rage and insolence as Winifred.'

Bransby drew the corners of his mouth together with a reflective thumb and forefinger, shaking his head slightly.

'I am much distressed by Winifred's treatment of you, Lydia; but, indeed, my dear, I think you will only make it worse by interfering.'

'I am sorry that you consider my sisterly interest interference, Godfrey,' replied Mrs. Crosdill, turning

inward her thin lips and puncturing the heavy velvet
with a force which had in it a hint of viciousness.

Poor Bransby was beginning to feel helpless.  He now
said almost pleadingly :

'Don't say that, Lydia ; you hurt me very much.'

'My dear Godfrey,' returned his sister, rising and
beginning to sort and put away her silks and bullion,
'the wholesome truth frequently hurts—in fact, nearly
always—but I shall certainly try to meet your wishes
in this respect, as in every other.  However, I can
think of nothing that would please me so much as
for you to have a long quiet talk with Bishop Cammersell about the position of a man in his household
and the education of children.  You would find him
delightful, so learned and cultivated, a prominent religious author, and a man of wide experience.  He is
not dictatorial.  I cannot imagine a more gentle, winning, Christ-like personality.  He has nine daughters
of his own, and has passed through burning ordeals.
The death of his devoted wife was a blow which I fear
has shattered his constitution.  I cannot tell you what
he was to me when Dabney died.  Such patience !

Such wonderful power of uplifting consolation ! And
then so practical in his advice—so wise in his views
of life and resignation ! I feel that it would be difficult
for one who lived daily in his atmosphere of calm
holiness to refrain from idolizing such a character. I
received a letter from him which was forwarded from
Florida only to-day, and which is full of that godly
spirit pervading his whole life. If you would care to
read it——'

She paused, and took up a little morocco box which
was always beside her, near her work-basket. It contained
her Bible, prayer-books, religious poems culled from
newspapers, the last tracts, and to-day the letter of Bishop
Cammersell, who was Bishop of a distant State in which
Mrs. Crosdill had lived during the years of her marriage.

' I should be delighted,' Bransby assured her, stretching
out his hand for the letter, which was written on large
sheets of ruled paper. The handwriting was squarely
round, and here and there tremulous.


' My DEAR FRIEND AND SISTER,' so ran the Bishop's
epistle, ' I have long been meaning to write and tell

you of my earnest approval of your noble and unselfish
work among the unenlightened children of Florida.
Surely this cup of cold water will bring you ample
reward, both in the future life and now also, in the
gratitude and love of these little ones, who must have
already learned to look up to you with loving gratitude.
Ah, how the heart aches when we are forced to ponder
upon the souls of thousands of children, as willing and
ready to drink in salvation as these which you are
leading to our blessed Master, and which are yearly
claimed by darkness—yes, lost for ever, because we do
not lay enough stress upon that solemn command to
preach the Gospel to every creature! I cannot tell
you, my dear friend and fellow-worker in the great
vineyard, how gratified and encouraged I am by the
success of your brave mission among these poor in-
fants, nor how earnestly I pray, night and morning,
that God may bless and prosper your efforts. That
you may see how sadly even our most civilized towns
are in need of like missions, however, I will relate to
you a most sorrowful case which took place under my
own eyes. It was that of a young girl, a sempstress,

who had long worked for my family, who had indeed just finished the mourning of my poor children for their sainted, beloved mother. Forgive this uncertain chirography. I cannot yet allude to my dear, dead saint without terrible agitation. However, to return to the story of poor Lucy Andrews. She had been coughing all winter (indeed, I had often remarked how ill she looked to Nelly, who used to make her beef-tea with her own hands during her last illness), so that it was scarcely a surprise to me when I finally heard that she was dying. Well, I went to see the poor girl. She had been a faithful, hard-working creature, had sent her two brothers to school with her earnings, and had housed an unfortunate but repentant Magdalen for over a year, and reclaimed her, by loving persistency, from the ways of sin. She also gave in many small ways, of which others had told me, for she was very shy and retiring, and would never have spoken to me of such matters on her own account. When I began to question her about her religious beliefs, however, I found, to my consternation and grief, that this poor creature had never been able to believe in the Divinity

of Christ, except, as she said to me, that He was nearer
God than anyone who had ever lived. All night
I remained with her in prayer, but, struggle as she
might, she could not seem to accept this vital fact.
Oh, my friend! God grant that you may never be
called upon to witness such a scene! She would cling
to my hand and sob piteously, and moan aloud, " Oh,
Bishop! Bishop! *make* me believe it! I cannot! I cannot! I love Him! I have always tried to do as He
said, but I cannot believe that He was God, in the
way you tell me I must believe. Oh, Bishop! do you
think that my soul will be lost if I can't believe it?
Do you think I will never see mother and my dear
Jack again?" (The poor girl was here alluding to her
betrothed, a young fellow named John Newin.) My
friend, what could I say? I knew that except through
Christ there was no salvation. The words, " Believe
on the Lord Jesus Christ, and thou shalt be saved,"
kept rising before me. I repeated them to her again
and again. It was useless. She expired with wild cries,
shrieking that she loved Him, but could not believe in
Him.

'Think, then, my sister, of what you may be doing for the young souls who gather about you every Sabbath; you might even read them this account of poor Lucy, if you think it would serve to impress upon them the lesson of Christian faith. My daughters and myself join in sincere thanks for the delicious bananas which came exquisitely packed in the gray Southern moss. How beautiful is its Indian name, " the curtains of death!" and how sombre are those actual curtains when through them we do not see the light of Christ shining gloriously, as it must always shine for true believers!

'Your faithful friend and brother,

'LIONEL CAMMERSELL.'

'A very striking, noble letter,' said Bransby, folding it and returning it reverently to its long envelope. 'That last figure about the " curtains of death" was most powerful. He seems to be a man of imagination as well as of deep religious quality, and his praise must be very gratifying to you, Lydia. It is indeed a good work that you have been doing.'

'I try to give my widow's mite,' Mrs. Crosdill said deprecatingly. 'It is all I have. Ah, Godfrey, how I should like to do for Winifred what I have been doing for those little strangers! I have not yet questioned her on her religious belief, but from her way of speaking I fear she is in outer darkness, to a great extent. She has no idea of reverence whatever. The other day I found her teaching her pug dog how to sit up on a volume of Taylor's sermons. But about the Bishop, if you cared to see him! He passes by here soon, on his way to Ashleigh, where you know he has a winter home, the climate of his own State being very trying. Suppose you were to ask him to stop for a day or two? I think that you would find his effect upon Eunice truly marvellous——'

'Er—if you would let me show her his letter,' said Bransby, somewhat hesitatingly, 'it could not help striking her——'

'Oh, his command of English is conceded to be wonderful, by everyone who hears him preach. His illustration and simile are really extraordinary. He might even be persuaded to give us a sermon, if he stayed over Sunday. Of course, I shall only be too delighted for you to show this letter to Eunice. It may throw a more favourable light upon my own character.'

Here she turned her lips inward again, and stiffened the muscles of her throat in a gesture of scornful indifference.

'My dear Lydia, I am sure that Eunice has a very high idea of your admirable qualities!' exclaimed Bransby nervously. 'But, of course, such a letter could but increase your most ardent admirer's good opinion of you. I will take it to her now.'

'Well, I pray that it may bring forth good fruit, Godfrey,' she returned, brushing her cold cheek along his in that contact which to them represented a kiss. 'And now good-night, as I shall have gone when you come back. Pray slip the Bishop's letter under my door when Eunice has read it.'

'Yes; good-night,' said Bransby. 'I hope very much that he can come. His letter is certainly most powerful and attractive. I will let you know at breakfast to-morrow about inviting him.  It depends only upon Eunice's health, I assure you.'

' Good-night,' repeated Mrs. Crosdill briefly, taking no notice of his last remark, except by a slight movement of one corner of her mouth.

# XXIII.

EUNICE was very amiable about the Bishop's letter, commended his sympathy with Mrs. Crosdill, said how sad was the fate of Lucy Andrews, and admitted that the figure about the Indian moss was calculated to impress a congregation very deeply. She agreed at once to send the desired invitation, and in response to it Bishop Cammersell appeared promptly at The Poplars. When he entered the house his fair skin was faintly reddened by his drive in an open trap through the stinging air, and his large violet, benign eyes looked out from eyelashes frosted with cold moisture. He was very tall and of a fragile build, and had white curling hair, which grew rather long, and fell about his face in gentle ecclesiastical ringlets. His large, rather bonelessly-modelled nose overdrooped a full mouth with deeply-pointed upper lip, the other melting into the curve of a slightly retreating chin. He had those long, white, easily-moving hands which the world somehow associates with distinguished Bishops, and his finely-modulated voice had a way of falling softly at the end of his sentences. Mrs. Crosdill had asked to go to the station to meet him, and was now assisting him to remove his heavy great-coat, and to shake the snow from his hat. Winifred, in her best frock, with a sheer white pinafore over it, backed slowly down the long hall, silently comparing the real Bishop to his black and white likeness.

It struck Eunice that she had never seen her sister-in-law so animated. There was a bright purplish spot of colour under her prominent eyes, and her gestures seemed suddenly to have grown more natural and vivacious.

Lois, a pretty, olive-eyed dumpling, sat solemnly in a carved chair by the chimney-corner, with her plump legs straight in front of her, and a Maltese kitten grasped firmly by the throat.

' How charming this great round hall is, with its big

fireplace and tapestry curtains !' said the Bishop genially.
' How very kind of you to ask me here, Mrs. Bransby !
Our greatest pleasures always come unexpectedly. Don't
you find it so ?'

' Oh yes—yes, indeed ! How wonderfully true !' exclaimed Mrs. Crosdill.

Eunice found the Bishop's talk much more natural and
attractive than his letter-writing. Watching his face
when Mrs. Crosdill addressed him, she decided that her
sister-in-law sometimes bored him with her enthusiastic
acquiescence in his least remark.

The Bishop, in the meanwhile, was charmed with
Eunice's frail loveliness and the blossom-like beauty
of her two children. Bransby also seemed to him very
agreeable. Altogether, it was one of those sudden and
congenial intervals in a petted prelate's existence.

' Well, my child,' he said, addressing Winifred as she
ventured to approach, clasping a small tulle-arrayed doll
in one brown little hand, ' is that your favourite daughter,
and are you bringing her up in the way in which she
should go ?'

' I don't know,' said Winifred. ' She's very ill—she's

broke her leg.' And she turned her child's voluminous skirts over her head, displaying a pink calico nudity and two china legs in painted black boots, one of which had been broken at the stout ankle.

Mrs. Crosdill suppressed a cry of shocked modesty.

' Winifred ! *Winifred !*' she exclaimed in a harsh whisper.

But the Bishop, taking the doll into his own hands, composed her ruffled skirts, and said that the best thing in the world for a broken leg was to have the severed foot restored to it by a strong glue.

' Yes, but you see it's lost,' replied Winifred gloomily.

' Then make one of sealing-wax,' said the Bishop cheerily. ' I've often done that for my little girls. Bring me a bit of black sealing-wax and I will heal your daughter at once.'

' Oh, dear Bishop ! How *charming* of you !' exclaimed Mrs. Crosdill. ' Winifred, my dear, if you will run up to my room, you will find a stick of black sealing-wax on my writing-table.'

Winifred scampered up the shallow oak stairway, which opened inviting arms just opposite the hall fireplace, and soon returned with the sealing-wax. Then the others gathered around while the Bishop carefully modelled an impossible foot and adjusted it to the broken ankle. Only Eunice remained quietly in her low chair near the fire, her eyes upon its mellow core, her hands twisting a little glass screen framed in silver. She felt wearily apart from all this orthodox gaiety. Bishop Cammersell had ordained the clergyman who had united her to Bransby. She was thinking with great bitterness of her married life. It seemed more a farce than usual to her just then. She felt herself smiling.

'My dear Mrs. Bransby,' said the Bishop, rising and coming over beside her, '"a penny for your thoughts," as my daughters say to me. You were evidently recalling some agreeable reminiscence.'

Eunice decided in a flash that the Bishop was uncomprehending, but answered simply :

'I am very glad that you could come, Bishop, but perhaps the drive in an open carriage was too cold for you.'

'Oh no. I like plenty of fresh air, and Mrs. Crosdill almost smothered me in fur robes. How very lovely this country is! What an ideal home you have here!'

'We are very fond of it,' said Eunice. 'My husband bought it from the Nelsons, and remodelled it in the colonial style. The staircase is taken bodily from an old English house of the time of Charles II.'

'And beautiful it is, too!' exclaimed the Bishop, putting on his glasses to observe the carving more minutely. Then he started up with an exclamation. 'But whose photograph is that? Surely—but no—and yet what a likeness! I used to know a young girl so like that—Barbara Cabell—but——'

Eunice's face grew vivid in a heart-beat.

'It is Barbara Cabell!' she exclaimed. 'Only she is married. Her name is Dering now—Barbara Dering. Did you really know her as a young girl, Bishop?—and did you think her as lovely then as she is now?'

'She was thinner,' said the Bishop reflectively, 'and she wore her hair brushed straight back from her forehead. She is more beautiful in this picture than I remember her.'

Eunice could not help flashing a glance at Mrs. Crosdill, whose face wore a look of sudden disapprobation.

'You have not mentioned that this is her *second* marriage,' she observed tartly.

The Bishop started visibly.

'You see, the Bishop and I agree on the subject of second marriages, Eunice. There is something savage and unchristian in them—at least to our thinking.'

'I cannot realize that Barbara Cabell has been twice married,' said the Bishop slowly. 'What a brilliant creature she was, to be sure! As vivid and untamed as a hawk, but wonderfully intelligent! I liked the child. Others found much fault with her, I know, but somehow my heart always yearned over her.'

Eunice was absorbing these remarks with a full and quiet sense of the sting which they must hold for her husband and sister-in-law.

'I think you would like Barbara far better than ever, Bishop,' she said naturally. 'She has grown spiritually and mentally almost beyond my power to describe.'

'Indeed!' exclaimed the Bishop, with an air of unfeigned delight.

'I might as well tell you, dear Bishop,' here put in Mrs. Crosdill feverishly, 'that my brother and I do not agree with my sister-in-law in this opinion. I, for example, find that Mrs. Dering is very unfeminine in many ways, and more like a hawk than ever.'

'I will ask Barbara to dinner, and the Bishop shall judge for himself,' said Eunice, whereupon Mrs. Crosdill flushed darkly, but made no further remark.

## XXIV.

BARBARA and Dering (the latter had just returned from New York) accepted the invitation to dinner, and Barbara had a lustrous, gem-like beauty in her straight gown of white with its bands of darkest sable.

Dering paid her so many compliments on the way over, that when they arrived the usual clear pallor of her face was overlaid with a warm flush. The nape of her firm throat shone whitely under little tendrils of dark-red hair. Other tendrils escaped and floated back over the band of pearls, which lost itself under her heavy coils. There was a knot of Parma violets at her breast.

The good Bishop, who was as capital a judge of beauty as most of his brothers, was enchanted.

'My dear child!' he exclaimed, enfolding her strong,

rose-tipped hand in both his own pale ones. ' How glad I am to see you looking so well and happy! Your charming friend, Mrs. Bransby, tells me, too, that you have improved as much in soul as in body during all these years. Ah, how well I remember your dear mother! You have her eyes—the same clear, honest, beautiful eyes. I am indeed overjoyed to see you again, my child, and under such happy circumstances!'

' Dear Bishop,' returned Barbara, in her rich, cordial voice, ' it is very nice of you to take such an interest in me!'

She pressed his hand gratefully, and felt herself more drawn to this simple, kindly, blue-eyed priest than to most others of his cloth. Dering, from a distant corner, eyed him critically.

' Oh Lord! it's another of those spoilt bishops!' he had exclaimed crossly, when Barbara showed him Eunice's invitation. ' For Heaven's sake, Bab darling, say you've got a finger-ache or something! Let's stay at home. By Jove! there's no bigger bore than this thing of bishopolatry.'

But she had persuaded him to come, drawing in gloomiest colours a picture of Mrs. Crosdill, and appeal- ing to his Christian charity to lighten poor Eunice's burden, if only for one evening.

She and Eunice soon fell into close conversation, while Mrs. Crosdill, a little apart, worked with aggressive con- centration at her conspicuously ecclesiastical embroidery, and the men grouped themselves before the roaring hickory fire—Dering with his legs firmly planted, one hand pulling at his short moustache, the other thrust deep into his trousers-pocket; the Bishop sunk into a huge leather chair, his delicate hands dangling tassel- like from either of his arms; Bransby standing in an attitude of hereditary composure, with one hand thrust under the tails of his rigidly smart evening coat.

' Now about our missions, Bishop,' burst forth Dering suddenly. ' Bransby tells me you are interested in missions. I was talking to a friend the other day— a friend who's in the Senate and up in such things— and he tells me that nearly all the troubles in China and the Hawaiian Islands have been occasioned by our

missionaries. They make a row and incite the natives
to rebel, and then they murder some authority or other,
and the Government sends down a gunboat and bom-
bards the island. I must say that I agree with Law-
rence Oliphant in thinking that one thing's awfully
needed nowadays, and that's a " missionary to the missionaries." '

The Bishop hastened to answer.

' My dear sir !' he exclaimed, ' if the world had
listened to such tales, where would our religion be
now ?   The Government often exaggerates at the expense of the Church.   But, then, I am an enthusiast on
the subject of missionary work.   I may express myself
too warmly.'

' I can't help thinking that missions, being the truest
sort of charity, should begin at home,' said Dering.
' But then, of course, I don't know anything really.
Only I can't help rather sympathizing with " H. H."
in her feeling about the Indians. It seems to me that,
after the shabby way in which we have treated them,
we owe them all our missionaries at least. I have
spent some time in the West, and the way in which

those poor devils—— I beg your pardon, sir!—but really, the way those poor chaps were cheated by the Government agents was infernal!—I do beg your pardon! It always makes my blood boil so to think of it that I don't seem to be able to choose my words.'

'Indeed, you are most excusable. I can quite comprehend your feelings,' said the Bishop pleasantly, ' but I cannot help thinking that your generous enthusiasm is somewhat wasted on those savage outcasts.'

' In my opinion,' said Bransby slowly, ' the Indian is a low, treacherous, unredeemable being, who should be exterminated as soon as possible.'

' Ah, no, my friend, I cannot say that I endorse that view of the subject,' objected the Bishop. 'They are certainly discouraging subjects for regeneration, but some noble work is being done among them. However, I understand very well Mr. Dering's feeling about the need of missions nearer home. You will remember, my dear Mrs. Crosdill, that letter I wrote you about poor Lucy Andrews. Surely that was a case for earnest missionary work.'

'Ah, yes, indeed!' exclaimed Mrs. Crosdill. 'That was terrible, terrible! I woke with a start only last night, haunted by your graphic description of that poor girl's cries. What a tragedy! A noble soul like that lost for ever from the mere lack of proper spiritual training!'

'What was this sad story, Bishop?' asked Barbara, coming suddenly forward, her lips parted in that eager forgetfulness of self which to some people made her face so irresistible. At her request, the Bishop repeated the sorrowful end of Lucy Andrews. As he went on, a look of suppressed excitement gathered in Barbara's wide eyes, and when he had finished speaking she exclaimed:

'But surely, Bishop, you didn't let the poor girl die in the belief that she was going to everlasting torment?'

The Bishop, sharply astonished, paused a moment before replying.

'My dear Mrs. Dering,' he then said, 'the idea cannot be more painful to you than it was to me; but what alternative was there? Soothing equivocations are not to be spoken in the room of death.'

' Is it possible,' said Barbara, a sort of horror welling into her face as she spoke—' is it possible that you really believe she went to hell—such a good, dear, loving soul as you describe her to have been !—just because something in her mind could not accept the letter of the law ?'

' And pray, my dear Mrs. Dering, what would you have done in my place, had you been a Bishop?' he demanded loudly, whereat a faint titter was heard to come from behind Mrs. Crosdill's embroidery-frame, and Bransby shifted his position a little uneasily.

' I should have told her that God is love !' cried Barbara, her face glowing. ' I should have said to her, " Poor child, whether you can believe these details or not, do you think that God will be less merciful to you than men? It is with the *heart* that man believeth unto righteousness—with the *heart* that we love." And "love is the fulfilling of the law." If she loved the Saviour, she believed in Him in the deepest sense of the word. I heard a sermon once by a Lutheran preacher, and he said such a good thing about that. " When you say that you believe in a man," he said, "in Emerson, for instance, do you mean to say that you believe that his mother was a Miss So-and-so, or his father a lawyer in a particular town at the time of his birth, or that he was born on a certain day of a certain year? No! You mean that you believe in his teachings, his philosophy, his theory of life—in a word, you believe in a man, not in the details of his birth ; and if you believe in the words of Christ and try to do His will and love His beautiful personality, you believe in Him, far more worthily than any orthodox Christian who accepts every historical detail relating to His appearance among men and yet hardens his heart to his fellows !" '

As Barbara spoke her face got paler and paler until it shone with a sort of white radiance from within. The Bishop, who, although undeniably rather vain and over-petted, had a kind heart and a very clear sense of justice, had come to the conclusion, during Barbara's little speech, that her fervour was prompted by real enthusiasm, not by a perverse desire to oppose her un-conventional ideas to his orthodox teachings. He said with gentleness, after a slight pause :

'Well, my dear, you must remember that I am an Episcopal Bishop. " Believe on the Lord Jesus Christ, and thou shalt be saved "—that is what I am ordained to preach at all costs, even though my soul is torn with pain in so preaching.'

Barbara came nearer, and finally seated herself on a low chair near the Bishop's, so that her attitude had in it something childlike and winning.

'But, dear Bishop,' she said, when he had stopped speaking, 'if to love God with one's whole being and one's neighbour as one's self are the foundation-stones on which rest all the law and the prophets, surely, surely, this poor Lucy, who told you over and over how she loved the Saviour, and who had loved a poor sinning outcast as herself—surely, because she could not believe in the orthodox sense of the word, you do not think her soul lost for ever?'

' My child,' returned the Bishop, ' I appreciate the loving-kindness of your own heart, which prompts you to plead so eloquently for this poor girl. But God's ways are past finding out. She died in unbelief. The Church has but one opinion for those who die in that manner.'

'God is love,' said Barbara; 'love forgives, for ever and ever.'

'And yet, my dear, there is an unpardonable sin.'

'Ah, yes!' exclaimed Barbara, starting to her feet. 'I have always thought that the unpardonable sin was the belief that there was any sin which God's love would not pardon.'

'My child! my child!' said the bishop warningly; 'take care that your mercy-loving and enthusiastic nature does not carry you into great error. Works without faith cannot avail—rather, they have the nature of sin, as it is said in the thirteenth article of our religion —because of the very fact that they are done without true piety; that is, without belief in the divinity of our Lord.'

'But surely right is right, and wrong is wrong, Bishop, no matter who does either. If a man who had been a thief all his life were to restore a jewel that he had stolen, that one act would remain righteous, even though he were to go on stealing jewels the next day. And although a man were an orthodox believer and the most rigid of Christians, as far as faith went, and yet were to kill his brother, the crime would remain a crime. Would it not? There are so many things which hurt me in our religion—things which seem to me so wrong, which I cannot admire or respect. Now, for instance, in our little church here in this neighbourhood there are some tables on which the Commandments are written, and every child or poor ignorant person can spell out for themselves every Sunday the terrible words, " For I the Lord thy God am a jealous God, and visit the sins of the fathers upon the children, unto the third and fourth generation." Yet who would ever think of setting up the tables inscribed with God's own contradiction of those words?—that eighteenth chapter of Ezekiel, which so few seem to know. I would give such a set of tables, oh, so willingly! and yet I am sure that I should not be permitted to do it. Wait till I get Eunice's Bible and show you the verses which I would select.' She brought the book, and read eagerly : ' " Yet say ye, Why? doth not the son bear the iniquity of the father? When the son hath done that which is lawful and right, and hath kept all my statutes, and hath done them, he shall surely live. The soul that sinneth, it shall die. The son shall not bear the iniquity of the father, neither shall the father bear the iniquity of the son : the righteousness of the righteous shall be upon him, and the wickedness of the wicked shall be upon him. But if the wicked will turn from all his sins that he hath committed, and keep all My statutes, and do that which is lawful and right, he shall surely live, he shall not die. All his transgressions that he hath committed, they shall not be mentioned unto him : in his righteousness that he hath done he shall live. Have I any pleasure at all that the wicked should die ? saith the Lord God : and not that he should return from his ways and live?" Ah, dear Bishop !' she ended, clasping her hands over the arm of his chair, and turning an eager face up to his, which was very puzzled and solemn, ' do let me give a set of tables with those words on it to some church in your diocese. I have so longed to do it. Please, please say yes !'

The Bishop looked as he felt, decidedly upset and un-comfortable.

' We shall see ! We shall see !' he murmured, letting

his eyes rove about, as though for some object which would, suggest a simile that might tide him over this direct and embarrassing appeal. 'Such a question could not be decided at once. It's a very serious matter—more so than you think, my dear. Such tables would offend many people, and be sure to wound the consciences of the weak brethren. But I shall reflect upon it, my dear. I shall certainly reflect upon it.'

Here Uncle Amos, appearing between the heavy tapestry *portières* which filled the great arch between the first and middle halls, said pompously :

' Dinner's purnounced, Miss Eunice.'

# XXV.

DURING dinner, Barbara, having seen that the feathers
of the worthy Bishop's soul were somewhat disturbed
by her eagerness, brought all her tact to the task of
soothing them again. She won him to relate his most
impressive anecdotes, appealed to him on literary matters,
and delighted him by her description of a clever little
niece of Martha Ellen's, who was only six years old, and
who could repeat, by heart and with fluency, the second
chapter of St. Matthew. Eunice could not decide
whether the Bishop was conscious of the effect which his
evident pleasure in Barbara's bright talk was producing
upon Mrs. Crosdill. That lady bridled, smiled now and
then to herself with demure bitterness, and tapped her
chest with a show of absent-mindedness which clearly
denoted her inward irritation.

Bransby and Dering were discussing the race question, so Eunice was at liberty to observe quietly all that passed, while she arranged a saucer of jelly for Win, who had been allowed to come down to dessert, and who was delightfully prim and self-important in a short-waisted white muslin frock tied with a pink ribbon, and wearing a little mob-cap on her dark curls. Having scraped up the last spoonful of the wine-sauce, which was served with the jelly, she said to her mother in a discreet whisper :

' Mother dear, I feel funny in my knees, but it's *very* cheerful.'

Eunice smiled and nodded over the orange which she was peeling.

Presently Win whispered again :

' I think Aunt Lydia's crosser 'n usually 'cause the Bishop's preachin' his whole sermon to Barbara.'

Eunice could not help smiling again, but touched her lips with her finger in a pantomime of the worn saw about children being seen and not heard. As the conversation grew more animated, however, Winifred urged :

'I just *must* tell you this, mother : I *do* think the Bishop's a little unpolite 'bout takin' the best things. He always took the best piece of celery, and now he's tooken the biggest banana. Do you think God will punish me for thinking His Bishop a little teeny weeny bit greedy?'

'Hush, Win,' said Eunice gravely, though she had more desire than ever to smile. 'You are getting saucy. You must try to get over that way you have of criticising older people. It's very improper in a little girl.'

'But, mother dear, isn't the truth as truly true when a little girl thinks it 'bout a bishop as when a bishop thinks it 'bout a little girl ?'

'Yes; but it's the Bishop's duty to tell little girls their faults, while it would only be disrespectful if little girls told bishops what they thought were their faults.'

'Well, is it disrespectful if I can't help liking Barbara's husban' better, and he ain't a bishop ?'

'No; that's no harm. But hush, dear, you're talking too much.'

Win began to eat her orange section by section,

plunging her little crimped teeth into the clear yellow
fibres, and curling her red lips away from contact with
the stinging juice. As she ate each division she placed
the seed, with the dainty deliberation peculiar to her,
along the edge of her plate. The Bishop, happening to
glance up, watched this operation with the sympathetic
smile of a somewhat sentimental father.

' Was it not a sweet thought of our heavenly Father
to make such delicious fruit for us all to enjoy, my
child ?' he asked at last.

Win gazed frankly at him over her last bit of
orange.

' But He made poison-berries an' things, too,' she
replied abruptly. ' Why do you reckon He did, sir ?'

' They are not poisonous to the birds of the air, who
live upon them, my dear.'

' Well, parsley kills parrots,' said Win. ' 'Cause we
had a parrot, and it ate it, and then it died in a hurry.
But of course I know "He doeth all things well,." sir,'
she hastened to add, fearing she was being disrespectful, and noting, besides, with a child's quick intuition,
the cloud of annoyance that was gathering on the

Bishop's brows and the anger brewing in the eyes of her aunt.

When Barbara and Dering were once more in their snug brougham on their way home, he suddenly caught her to him and laced her arms close about his throat.

'There! for Heaven's sake let me feel the contact of something warm, reviving, human! I've been talking abstractions with that lump of frozen dough, Bransby, until my marrow feels about to congeal! Your lips, Barbara, before I turn into marble, like the chap in the "Arabian Nights." '

Outside, the fields were smooth with snow and the sky like the inside of an onyx globe, set with sharp, many-coloured diamonds. It was very cold, and the window-panes were soon frosted with their breath.

Dering laughed, and wrote Barbara's name with his finger upon the blurred glass.

'There! that's typical. I always see the world through that medium!' And again he kissed her.

'But how terrible for poor Eunice to be shut up in that country-house all winter with Bransby and his sister!' said Barbara after awhile. 'She is a goddess of patience. I couldn't stand it.'

'You!' Dering laughed at the idea. 'I can fancy you giving that would-be Mrs. Bishop a piece of your mind. What a terror she is—worse than the man! But I like Eunice much better than I ever did.'

Barbara was delighted, and put her left hand upon his, in which her right was already clasped.

'How glad I am!' she exclaimed. 'She is a wonder, but so quiet that most people don't understand her, and are apt to think her weak. She has always liked you.'

Dering could not help grinning a little as he answered :

'She has a great variety of tastes. She must have a genius for adapting herself to different characters, if she likes me and Bransby at the same time.'

'Oh, Jock! You must see, you must feel——' began Barbara, and then stopped, afraid of being disloyal to her friend. 'Eunice was so very, very young when she was married,' she added hastily.

'Poor soul!' exclaimed Dering. Then, taking Bar-

bara's face between his hands, he rested his lips upon
hers in a long, complete kiss of quiet intensity. 'There!'
he said, as he lifted his head. 'Just to think that she
has never been kissed like that in all her eleven years of
marriage! What a shame! And such an adorable
mouth as she has, too!'

Barbara smiled back into his half-mischievous eyes,
then, with a contented sigh, settled herself comfortably
against his side and rested her head upon his breast.
He had never seemed to her so charming, so much a
man, as thus contrasted with the pale and emotionless
Bransby. The movement of the firm muscles in his
arm, as he searched for his match-box to light a
cigarette, pleased her woman's pride in strength. She
could not understand at all how Eunice, even as a very
young girl, could have fancied Bransby, with his dapper,
incapable little figure, his smooth pale hair, his neat
beard, cut exactly in a point, his great light-brown eyes,
and thin, colourless lips. She thought of his tiny hands
and feet with a sensation of physical revulsion. Even
that fierce cruelty which is so often an excrescence of
strength was more acceptable to her than the frigid,

sexless calm of Bransby's conjugal manner. She recalled Mommsen's saying, that 'there is no genius
without passion,' and agreed with it vehemently. At
least Dering, with all his faults, was powerful, responsive, full of varied fire, and never roused in her that
sense of mental nausea which she felt convinced must
have sometimes overpowered Eunice in the presence of
Bransby's tepid platitudes about heaven, life, and duty,
all three of which he could only know as quotations
from highly orthodox and conventional volumes. He
himself reminded her of a paragraph from a religious
novel. This last fancy made her laugh out and press
her head with a childishly affectionate gesture against
Dering's shoulder, kissing the stuff of his coat as she
did so.

'Darling!' he said, charmed. 'But why did you
laugh? What were you thinking of?'

She told him, and they were merry at Bransby's
pious expense for some moments. The glare from the
moonlit snow glimmering in at the carriage windows
lighted up their faces with a pale glow, and they could
see each other's white teeth flashing gaily. A sense

of youth and vigour stirred them both. They grasped
each other's hands so eagerly that it was almost painful,
and gazed at the windows, from which they brushed
the moisture now and then, with that excitement in
detail which possesses two children who are traversing a
strange country.

'How dim and blue the hills are! and how they
melt into the sky!' said Barbara. 'I feel so strong
and gay—just as though I could take your hand and
run over that bright snow for hours, without feeling
tired. Brr! *What* an odious dinner it was! How
dreadful most ecclesiastical anecdotes are!—don't you
think so?'

'Yes; the Bishop was much better than his stories,'
admitted Dering slowly, hindered from responding
wholly to her gaiety by that sudden feeling of religious
conventionality which sometimes overwhelmed him.
He allowed himself a certain license now and then in
speaking of the clergy, but resented it in others, even in
Barbara. It was the same feeling that makes mothers
ready to punish their children themselves, while they
get angry with anyone else who attempts to do so.

Barbara was too happy and gay to-night, however, to notice the negative tone in his voice, and went on eagerly :

' How beautiful it is ! How I love these rolling fields all swathed in snow ! They are like the breasts of Titanesses, with a red streak here and there that looks like blood.'

' Oh! oh !' cried Dering, in a shocked tone. ' What would Bransby say if he could hear you ? What an immodest simile ! How lacking in all womanly refinement !'

And again they laughed gaily.

' I'll tell you what,' said Dering, after a moment or two : ' Mrs. Crosdill is setting that hideous widow's cap of hers for the blue-eyed Bishop. She'll marry him, too !'

' Oh, Jock ! do you think so ? I fancy she bores him. And then with their horror of second marriages——'

' Horror of fiddlesticks !' retorted Dering. ' They'll put it on a high moral and religious platform. You see if they don't ! She will marry him to be a mother to his —nine daughters did he say ?'

'And he?' asked Barbara. 'What will he marry her for?'

'Oh, I dare say he'll suddenly become convinced of the positive command in that verse, " A bishop *must* be the husband of one wife." You know there are people who take it that way.'

'How glad I am that you are not a bishop!' Barbara exclaimed frivolously. 'I couldn't help feeling as if it were a sort of religious ceremony whenever you kissed me.'

Their moods were mutually sympathetic to-night. To Dering she seemed perfection, in her simple white gown with the little furze of red-gold strands outlining her fine head. The violets at her breast gave forth a languid perfume, and the high collar of fur on her cloak accentuated the smooth clearness of her face. Her voice, rich and low, thrilled him as though he had heard it for the first time. He was more thoroughly in love with her than he had ever been, and ventured to kiss her throat with something of a lover's timidity.

She felt nearer to him than she had for a long time.

That air of husbandly assurance which she resented had entirely disappeared. They went to the music-room on reaching home, and Dering lay on the rug before the fire and smoked, while she played softly the different odds and ends that he loved best.

After awhile she stopped, and, coming over beside him, said :

' A penny, Jocko ! I can almost hear your thoughts.'

' I was thinking,' said Dering slowly, ' what hard luck it is that everyone isn't as happy as I am. And then I was trying to realize that there were people to-night who, in addition to mental suffering, were cold and hungry. It seems hideous.'

' It is hideous,' said Barbara. ' Sometimes I wonder so about it all. I would be so willing to give all I had to the poor, if I really thought that it would be anything but a penny dropped in mid-ocean. How I should love to see you a great philanthropist, darling ! I have so often thought that a great work lay before you in that line.'

' How strange !' exclaimed Dering, lifting himself upon

his elbow and looking at her curiously. ' Gad, you *are* a witch —you wonder !'

' Is that what you have been thinking of ?' asked Barbara tenderly. Then she looked at him with her deep, loving eyes, and, resting one hand on his thick hair, said in a low voice : 'If you could think out some plans for lessening poverty and vice, I would be willing to give up everything and help you in your work. I mean even if you wished to live with the working classes, as Felix Holt did. Only '—she paused, and then went on seriously—' I don't believe in equality any more than I would love a world that is one vast level. There must be valleys and moun- tains in human nature, as well as in landscapes. People are happier for looking up. What I long for is that everyone should have the blessing of happy work and ample earning. But that idea of living in droves is horrible to me. It would make of life one vast American hotel. I don't think anyone who had a touch of the artist in him could ever have imagined such a system. The very monotony of it would pall on one. I really think I'd rather be a jolly tramp, with a certain amount of exciting doubt as to how I should get my dinner, and where I should sleep that night.'

Dering smiled, and, taking her hand from his hair, pressed its palm against his lips a little absently.

' " The destruction of the poor is their poverty," ' he said at last. ' Of that I am convinced. But how to help it—how to help it !'

He was silent again, and sat gazing into the flameless fire.

' Do you think of making it a life-work, dearest?' she asked, after some moments. ' How happy that would make me !' Her face lighted up. ' Oh, Jock, how happy we should be if you thought of that !' she cried again. ' I would be with you in everything—even in the most quixotic things that you might do. If you were to give away all our money, you would never hear me murmur.'

Dering looked at her with a rare moisture in his eyes.

' Oh, Barbara,' he said, ' if that poor devil Lydgate, in " Middlemarch," had had a wife like you ! It seems

to me that you are the only entirely comprehending
woman I ever knew.  I am sure you are the only woman
who never has any petty jealousies.'

'I could not care for anyone unless I had absolute
faith in him,' she said proudly.  'Women who weep
or make scenes because their husbands unexpectedly
spend a night away from home are beyond my compre-
hension.  Either I believe in my husband or I do not.
If I believe in him, surely there is no need of watching
him and making his life a burden, by requiring from him
an account of every moment he has spent away from me.
If I don't believe in him, what difference does anything
else make?'

'You dear, big-hearted, big-minded, big-souled darling!'
exclaimed Dering.  He knelt up and put both arms
about her.  'You have forgiven me entirely, haven't
you, dearest?' he whispered.

'Oh, my dear! how can you ask?'

She kissed his eyes and forehead, and stroked lovingly
his boyish curls.

Suddenly they discovered that they were hungry, and
Dering suggested that they should go to the store-room

and see if there were anything to eat. These midnight raids on the larder they found delightful, and often chattered over an impromptu feast of this sort until nearly one o'clock. Barbara now lighted one of the tall silver candlesticks that stood on the piano, and they went through the dining-room and opened the door into the little arched way which led to the store-room. As soon as they passed out, a gust of wind whipped the candle-flame down to a blue fleck, and the dogs began to bark angrily. Barbara held her skirts nervously about her, while Dering tried to fit the key into the lock. She dreaded that sudden, panting rush of the dogs, which always made her heart jump so foolishly.

At last they got the store-room door open, before the dogs reached them, and were at once enveloped in that peculiar musty odour of cheese, apples, jam, bread, potatoes, meal, cold meat, which pervades all store-rooms. Then Barbara held the candle while Dering scrambled upon a flour-barrel and investigated the top shelf. He found a huge rosy pear, handed it down to her, and at once she thrust her teeth deep into the juicy flesh, with a little cry of pleasure, dancing

about with her mouth full, like a merry school-
girl.

Dering, from his perch on the flour-barrel, gravely
admonished her.

' You, " a wife and a mother," as the novels put it, to
be capering about like a madcap! What would your
last admirer, the Bishop, say? Cease, cease, I 'beseech
you, madam, this unseemly conduct, and have the grace
to leave me as much of that pear as Eve left Adam of
the apple.'

' Here, you can have all the rest!' cried Barbara,
holding up the closely-nibbled core.

But Dering was occupied in tearing away great
crackling bites from a crisp, wine-sap apple, and did not
notice this generous offer.

They found a round, crimson cheese, some cold turkey,
a bunch of celery, a jug of hard cider, and a great loaf of
brown bread, and with this booty returned to the dining-
room, where, chattering like two affectionate magpies,
they spread some napkins over the green cloth, arranged
plates, and placed knives, spoons, and forks, Barbara
rushing into the greenhouse at the last moment, and

bringing in an azalea-bush in full flower, ' to make things pretty,' as she said.

As she ate, with that dainty carefulness that Dering loved, he watched her, more enchanted than ever. The little gurgling noise which the cider made in flowing down her throat, and which might have irritated him in an unloving mood, seemed to him the most charming thing in the world. The dewy-red of her lips, her pretty way of lading her slice of bread with little morsels of the gold-coloured cheese, then nibbling it fastidiously with the points of her small teeth—all this seemed to him as individual, and therefore as delightful, as her hair, her eyes, her voice, her way of speaking. He could not realize that he had ever been angry with her, and she looked so thoroughly the girl, as she sat with her hair hanging loose about her shoulders, that he found it hard to believe that their child lay sleeping upstairs, only the hall's length from their own bedroom.

## XXVI.

THE unpleasant emotion which had risen in Dering on learning that Barbara was to have a child, and which he called by various names, but never by its true one, jealousy, had been latent for several weeks. Barbara, in her position of mother, seemed to him astonishingly reasonable. He had expected her to merge her individuality into that of the little Fairfax, to be nervous about the baby's health on all occasions, absent-minded and preoccupied when with him, a constant inmate of the nursery, in constant need of *tête-à-têtes* with the family doctor—in a word, the devoted mother, entirely at the expense of the companionable wife.

As none of these changes took place, he returned very soon to his normal state of mind, and even took a strange, humorous sort of pleasure in the child—its

queer little spasms of expression ; its faint and mysterious
sneezings, which sounded like the noise made by rose-
leaves popped on the back of one's hand ; its long
yawns, almost dislocating its tiny jaws ; its vague and
momentary opening of round black-blue eyes. All these
he found exquisitely droll ; and when, one day, he saw in
its small downy face a certain movement of the brows,
which was a direct inheritance from Barbara, he could
not contain a shout of amusement, which terrified Fair
into vigorous howlings.

About ten days after the Bransbys' dinner, however,
the baby was taken suddenly ill, and Poppleton, the
neighbouring doctor, had to be sent for at midnight.
As such things happen, the weather was very bitter,
roads and meadows iron-bound, with a black frost.
Dering detested cold, and was not over-amiable about
getting into his clothes and going out to one of the
cabins, to rouse Tobit and send him for the doctor—this
being necessary, as none of the servants, except Martha
Ellen and Aunt Polly, slept in the house, and they were
both busy over Fair.

An hour later Poppleton was at Rosemary. Dering

had come downstairs to. get some whisky, and was standing in his dressing-gown over an open register when the doctor entered. He was a huge man, of about forty-eight, with a smooth, dark-red face, on which no hair had ever grown, small dark-blue eyes set between thick folds of fat, like the seeds of some fruit in its pulp, and over which he wore gold-rimmed spectacles seemingly imbedded in a crease at the base of his nose. This feature was of indefinite outline, speckled with violet pores and inclining to the left. He had a handsome mouth, about which were deep, stationary dimples, large jaws, mottled with a vinous purple, and surmounting his high, oval forehead a dark-brown, much-curled wig. When he laughed, which was often, he disclosed splendid yellow-white overlapping teeth. He wore a faded plum-coloured coat, which was spotted orange, here and there, by spilt physic and red clay. His ponderous calves were strapped into russet gaiters, and between his shoulders he carried a great leather-covered medicine-chest. His hands, handsome and glazed with fatness, had broad, bitten nails, over which the pink flesh curled back. His custom was to address each patient in the voice of some other, and he now began, in a high, quivering treble, which Dering instantly recognised as that of an old man in the neighbourhood who had turned Methodist preacher in his sixty-fourth year.

'So the little heiress of Rosemary has the croup?' he trilled forth, with perfect mimicry. 'May the Lord see fit to aid my poor efforts! For 'tis not in my physic-box alone to succour her. Alas! if such——'

'Do shut up, doctor, and come along,' said Dering curtly. As a rule he was 'great friends' with Poppleton, who amused him vastly, but to-night, in addition to his real anxiety about the child, he felt that he had caught cold and was not in a responsive mood.

The doctor, who thoroughly understood and liked him, smiled good-naturedly, and began to mount the stairs, planting each great creaking foot softly with the air of an elephant attempting to walk on tiptoe. Dering followed, determined, as soon as the baby had been dosed, to ask for something to stop his cold. He gave a violent sneeze, just as they reached the nursery door, and resolved angrily that Tobit should be lodged in the house to-morrow, in case of future emergencies. As they entered the room they saw Fair striking out with her small fists, in her effort to breathe. Barbara was walking her up and down, a fixed expression on her pale face. A sudden throe of mother-love had seized her. She felt that, if the little creature on her breast were to die, it would be like tearing a piece of her heart away with forceps. Martha Ellen followed her, with cooing sounds of comfort, her great eyes bright with tears. Aunt Polly at the fire was warming another blanket, the scorched smell of which filled the room.

Somehow Dering felt aggrieved that, although he had taken a bad cold, no one spared him a thought, but seemed utterly absorbed in the croupy morsel which Barbara held with such an expression of dread on her face.

' Well, well, well, well, well !' murmured the doctor, unconsciously falling into the tone of Aunt Polly, who was now swathing Fair in the smoking blanket. ' Let me see ! let me see ! Now, honey, you cheer up right away !' he added, addressing Barbara suddenly. ' Here, give her to me ; we'll have everything all right in a minute or two. She'll be " jes' ez spry ez a black-snake with a new hoop-skirt," as old Tom Jinx says.' And here he adopted the voice and accent of another patient.

Dering sat grumpily resigned close to the fire, with one of the baby's blankets drawn closely about him an l over his ears. The shrieks of poor little Fair, th doctor's cheery jokes, the skurrying back and forth of Aunt Polly and Martha Ellen, all jarred more and more on his irritated nerves. Finally, when boiling wa'er was poured into a bucket filled with lumps of lime, and the room dim with puffs of the penetrating steam, he could stand it no longer, and said that, as he could be of no use, he would go to his room, and the doctor must come after him if he was needed, or if he, Popple-ton, wanted anything. He built a huge fire, wrapped himself in more rugs, and, filling a tumbler with hot water and whisky, established himself in an arm-chair with a volume of Greek history.

He was deep in the education of the young Spartans, and wondering if Spartan babies ever had croup, when Poppleton entered simultaneously with his knock,

wiping his pendulous chin and the back of his huge
neck with a flowered handkerchief.  He nodded cheerily
at Dering, and called out in the tones of yet another
patient, a young fellow with a voice as ill-proportioned
to his size as that of a grasshopper, and who thought
himself a second Booth :

' 'Tis well, 'tis very well !   All works as I would
have it !   So !   Ha ! ha !'   Then, noticing Dering's unen-
couraging expression, he dropped into his natural manner,
and said easily : ' Little heiress getting along first-rate !
I see you're having a toddy this bitter night.   Thermo-
meter only two above zero.   I tell you 'twas cold riding
here !'                          .

The doctor's air was a masterpiece of unconsciousness,
but Dering poured him out four fingers of whisky, which
he drank at once with the mildness of a kitten lapping
milk.

' I say, doctor,' burst forth Dering abruptly, ' what
the devil's good for a cold ?   I've caught an infernal
one to-night, going out after someone to send for you.'

' Quinine, quinine, quinine !' chanted the doctor.

' But it makes my head buzz so,' objected Dering

crossly. ' Do show some originality in your prescrip-
tions! I've taken enough quinine for colds this winter
to stuff a pin-cushion, and I never found it did me any
good. For Heaven's sake try again.'

' Ten drops of camphor, then. Can you take camphor ?'
said the doctor, who was too fond of him to mind his
surface humours.

' I'll take anything,' said Dering, with gloomy reck-
lessness.

' Oh, ho ! don't I wish I'd had those fellers that
granted that charter for prize-fighting in Virginia in your
frame of mind!' returned Poppleton. ' Wouldn't I have
fixed 'em up with ten drops of vitriol and prussic acid
apiece !'

' Yes, I know. It's a disgrace to the State. But our
joint opinions on that subject aren't going to help my
cold, are they ?'

The doctor grinned, while dropping ten drops of camphor on a lump of sugar, and Dering proceeded to suck
it with that solemnity which pervades for us our personal
ailings. Poppleton could not help laughing at his serious
face.

' I'll tell you what,' said Dering, unmoved; ' if you had the colds I have you wouldn't see much humour in them.'

Before the doctor could reply, Rameses appeared at the door and beckoned him away.

Fair recovered from this attack, but was feverish and ailing for two weeks, during which time Dering saw scarcely anything of Barbara. His cold had proved rather severe, and he was in bed for a day or two, but Barbara could not spare enough time from Fair to read to him, and he lay in lonely discomfort, that aggrieved feeling which had come over him in the nursery growing ever stronger. They were both ill, he told himself, and while the child had two competent attendants, Barbara could not even tear herself away from it long enough to do more than irritate him by opening and shutting the door within such a short space of time. It was evident for which she felt more sympathy, more anxiety. Her very coldness at first was all the more reason that she should now become excessive in her fondness. All romance was over and done with ! He went on lashing himself into a sort of frenzy. He would hear of nothing now but croup, colic, teething, nurses, physics, change of climate! He flung himself angrily about, and finally lay still and stared at his reflection in a glass which stood at the foot of his bed.

His sallow face and the dark circles about his eyes filled him with a spasm of self-pity.

'By Jove! she can see me look as ill as that and keep away from me as she does! What a fool I was to build air-castles and actually fancy them granite! I suppose those cynical old chaps are right when they say that women are meant for mothers before everything else! What a come-down!'

He laughed, and the savage expression of his face in the glass struck him as perfectly appropriate to the present state of affairs.

One afternoon, ten days later, he and Barbara went for a ride. Wilful, Barbara's horse, of which she was so fond, was a lean, compact chestnut, with a delicate crest, splendid shoulders, long, elastic pasterns, and quarters that could lift him even over a snake-fence when not too exaggerated in height. His greatest

beauty was his head, tipped by slender ears, clear-cut
as though shaped with a pair of fine scissors.  His wide
front, splashed with a large white star, gave him a
gracious air, and his eyes were overarched by full brows,
on which was a darker pencilling.  He carried his tail
like a triumphant gold plume, and his mane shone like
ravellings of silk.  He was excitable, but entirely kind,
and knew Barbara as her dogs knew her.

Dering's mount was as different as possible.  A powerful half-bred bay, with a short barrel, head tapering too
abruptly to a small-nostrilled muzzle, pasterns short but
clean, and broad, well-shaped hoofs.  Dering rode him
with a bit and bridoon, while Wilful's bridle was a
single-reined snaffle, very light, yet with a thin bar
capable of hurting, and he also had on a noseband, as
he pulled a good deal when his blood was up.

Dering, still pale and fretful from his cold, fumed
about stirrups and saddle, while Barbara's mulatto groom
swung her up on Wilful, and Rameses fed him with
sugar to keep him quiet.

Dering was in a sore, sullen state of mind, and, more-
over, had determined that he would have it out with

Barbara during this ride, and put her love for him to the test. Her gaiety and delight in Wilful and his antics jarred on his nerves more every instant, especially as Wilful's whirlings and playful rearings and backings stung him now and then with anxiety for Barbara. It seemed to him, in his sulky mood, that she was reckless and inconsiderate, laughing aloud as Wilful swung her about in the saddle, and letting the reins give to their full length under the impatient movements of his neck.

As they began to canter down the long lawn, he gave way to his vexation, and cried rather crossly :

'If you can't make that beggar move decently ahead let's pull up to a walk !'

Wilful, in fact, was cantering sideways as deliberately as though he had been a gamesome crab, and Barbara, convulsed with merriment, was giving him his way. She saw that Dering was in a dangerous vein, and answered good-naturedly :

'Yes, I know it's awfully provoking, but I never can make him walk when he first starts.'

Dering grew more and more provoked, but was silent,

not wishing to give way to his anger before finding out the true state of her affections.

It was one of those perfect days which come so often in a Virginia winter. The air had the mingled warmth and freshness of early spring ; there were bits of young green here and there ; the fields undulated in a soft wind, and overhead was a curve of blue, across which frail clouds were swept as by a gigantic broom. The roads, spongy and yet not actually muddy from a light fall of snow, which was now thawing, were in excellent condition for galloping.

Wilful struck out into his graceful swinging stride, his neck, which was like iron cased first in india-rubber and then in satin, eagerly arched, his nostrils distended. Close to his flank the big bay, Standby, lumbered steadily. Somehow Barbara's evident delight in her horse fretted Dering. He was in a mood to resent any form of enjoyment in another. Her very exuberance of physical strength and radiance accentuated his own dragged-down condition and sensation of inertness.

' Er—I'm not feeling very fit,' he began, when they had settled into a trot along an uneven bit of road. ' I need some toning up, I fancy, and then, too, I'm getting pretty sick of doing nothing. It's an awfully lazy life that we've been leading.'

' Yes, I wish that you had some steady occupation, Jock,' answered Barbara brightly. ' I don't think that anyone can be really happy without it.'

' Well, there's a splendid chance for change of scene open to us,' said Dering, with an air of such intense unconsciousness that she at once decided he was about to propose some extraordinary scheme. ' I've had an invitation from Leland—you know, that fellow who's so interested in social questions—we were college chums. Well, he's going West on a sort of shooting and investigation tour combined—private car and all that. He wants us to go — you and me. Mrs. Leland's a charming little woman—crazy to know you. In fact, they're both awfully keen about your going.'

She looked at him earnestly.

' But Fair?' she asked finally. ' We couldn't drag a baby of that age along with us?'

' I should fancy not !' exclaimed Dering. ' I

certainly don't propose making nuisances of our-selves !'

Barbara thought that the invitation might have been given for a later date, and asked when they were expected to be ready.

'In ten days. They start from Washington on a Wednesday.'

She was silent for some moments, trying to comprehend whether really he wished her to leave the child so soon after its severe illness.

'Well,' he broke out impatiently, 'shall I write and accept, or do you think it would be better if you were to do it ?'

'Do you mean, Jock, that you wish me to leave Fair while she is so delicate ?'

'Delicate? Fiddlesticks ! You young mammas are like Chicken Little when the leaf fell on her back— she thought the sky was falling; and you go to pieces over a simple attack of croup ! I don't suppose there ever was a baby who didn't pull through attacks of croup more or less sharp. Julius Cæsar, Oliver Cromwell, Napo-leon Bonaparte, they all had it, I'd stake my life !'

'Fair didn't have a simple attack of croup, Jock. She had diphtheritic sore-throat, and is liable to other attacks like it, until the cold weather is over.'

'Oh, I might have known you'd make the worst of it all, just to avoid leaving her for a week or two! I must say you're about as "hoodooed" by your first-born as anyone I ever saw.'

Barbara flushed, then after a second said quietly :

'I think it's very natural that I should not want to leave her as weak as she is now.'

'There's Mrs. Bransby! She knows any amount more about babies than you do. Leave the brat with her!'

Barbara flushed still more, then grew pale.

'I shouldn't be satisfied to leave her with anyone. If she were to be very ill and I away enjoying myself, I should never get over it.'

'I suppose not. But I may be as ill as I like, and you don't ever see it, so long as that kid is ailing!'

Barbara gripped the edge of her saddle with her right hand in her effort for self-control.

'I thought you had only a bad cold,' she then said.

'Do you feel really ill? Have you kept anything from me?'

Her eyes had grown suddenly anxious. This touched him, and for the moment his tone was softer.

'Oh, there's nothing serious,' he assured her. 'I'm run down and seedy, that's all. But I feel the need of a change. Do ask Mrs. Bransby to look after the child, there's a darling, and come along with me!'

He leaned over and put an impulsive arm about her waist, and the horses, used to such manœuvres, nipped at each other with a friendly pretence of enmity.

She looked puzzled and worried, then turned her dark eyes on him appealingly, and said :

'Jocko, you know how much I'd like to go with you, but indeed, indeed, I feel that I cannot leave Fair just now.'

He withdrew his arm with angry roughness and touched Standby into a brisk trot. Wilful cantered airily a half-length ahead, and some bits of mud were thrown against Dering's shoulders.

'I wish you'd have the ordinary politeness not to

spatter me all over with mud from that confounded brute's heels !' he called out.

Barbara brought Wilful down to a trot also, but did not say anything. She felt sure that if her husband kept up that tone with her the discussion would end in a quarrel. Presently he began again :

' So you refuse, then, do you, to go with me, though I tell you I'm feeling wretchedly and need your companion- ship ! How I have heard you excoriate that trait in other women !' he laughed. ' Well, it's the old thing of a fellow-feeling making us wondrous kind, I suppose ! That's it ! Eh ?'

Barbara's lip trembled, but there were no tears in her eyes. She had long since learned to repress this sign of emotion, finding that in moods like this it only goaded Dering to further harshness.

' I don't see how you can put it that way, Jock,' she said at length, in a low voice, speaking all the more gently that she felt her own temper rising. ' I despise the lack of fire which makes women slight their husbands for their children as much as ever ; but duty is duty. When I see that a thing is right I must do it, or at least

I must try to do it. Don't you know that I would leave
Fair in a minute—in a second—to come to you if you
were seriously ill?'

Dering was silent, and continued to smile as though
over mysterious and enlightening thoughts.

'Speak, Jock! You know that!' cried Barbara,
growing impatient. 'At least you must acknowledge
that I've always been truthful. You must believe what
I say.'

'Well,' replied Dering slowly, 'I confess it's rather
hard to take in what you say to me with such opposite
facts staring me in the face.'

'What facts?' said Barbara. 'My child—our child
has been seriously, even dangerously, ill. I don't want
to leave her and go West for an indefinite length of time.
Are those the facts you mean? Is there anything in
that but what is womanly, natural, wifely?'

'Womanly and natural, I admit,' he sneered, 'but—
er—hardly what you could call wifely.'

'Would you really have me leave Fair?'

'With your friend Eunice? Assuredly.'

'And if she were to be very, very ill?'

' She would be in far better hands than those of an enthusiastic and ignorant young mother, who would probably keel over in a dead faint at the first bad symptom.'

' You are unjust!' flashed Barbara.

' My dear Bab, calling me names won't alter facts.'

' How can you love me, as you say you do, and yet speak to me like this?'

' Our ideas of love probably differ as much as our ideas of duty, my dear girl.'

' I cannot understand you!' she exclaimed. 'I cannot take in that you are really angry because I won't leave a poor, helpless, ill little baby to the care of others, when it is my simple duty to stay with her. But you're not my Jock this afternoon. You're in one of your black moods. I am sure you'll .see things differently to-morrow.'

' Are you?' he answered briefly, with a scowl and a grin together. ' Then it'll be a devilish good thing if you get that notion out of your head, as you're laying up a lively disappointment for yourself.'

'I wish you wouldn't use such expressions to me, Jock.'

'What d——d nonsense!' he retorted roughly. 'You're not over-squeamish yourself when your blood's up! Come, now, be honest about it! You know I caught you swearing the other day, or, if not swearing, using jolly strong expletives. Did you or did you not say, "Plague take the cusséd thing!" when you couldn't get your stirrup tight? Eh? Answer me that, my Lady Highty-Tighty!'

Barbara almost broke into a laugh, but her anger conquered, and she merely curled a disdainful lip in reply.

'Because I'll tell you what,' he fumed on—'"Plague take it!" is about as abominable an expression as could be used, when you come down to it. The plague is a filthy disease, and when you say those words you are calling it down on the object of your wrath!'

'Do you think that the plague could materially injure a stirrup-leather?' asked Barbara gravely. 'Because, if so, I will ask in my prayers to-night to be forgiven.'

'We'll let that go,' said Dering, who was now of a curious steely pallor. 'But at least you'll admit that "cusséd" is, to say the least, a vulgar, unladylike word; or perhaps you won't admit it?'

'Oh!' cried Barbara, with an air of disgusted weariness, 'I'll admit anything, if you'll only let me take the rest of my ride in peace.'

'There's another charming trait you've developed this afternoon!' he retorted. 'You are willing, then, to admit an untruth for the sake of your personal comfort! Jove! I *am* glad to know that. That'll save me a world of bother in future discussions.'

'I'm glad to know that I've helped you to a clearer knowledge of my character,' she replied, recklessly giving way to the temptation of sarcastic retorts.

Glancing at him, she was overcome with that sense of his ugliness which, during his fits of temper, seemed to her to blot out every vestige of good looks from face and figure. His whole presence revolted her. She shivered and settled herself more firmly in the saddle. 'If he will only content himself with sulking and let me alone!' she thought wearily. 'He does make me

so wicked! My tongue stings like an adder after he
has goaded me beyond a certain length of time. Oh,
if he will only let me alone! It is so horrible! When
he is like this I don't love him. I long to get away
from him. What have I done to rouse this mood in
him? Let me think.' She went over everything
that had passed between them for a month, but without arriving at any solution of his present frame of
mind.

'Of course you know what the world will say?' he
began, so abruptly that she started and changed
colour.

'What?' she asked, with some vagueness.

'Why, they'll say I'm tired of you, and in love with
Mrs. Leland.'

'Oh, Jock, how vulgar!' breathed Barbara, her eyes
full of disgust rather than anger. 'Don't you know
that if I could think such things of you I should stop
loving you?'

'I really don't know what you'd do under given
circumstances, my dear. You've turned out, in nearly
everything, the exact opposite of what you seemed before

marriage—cold, prudent, selfish, conventional, a baby-worshipper, a shrew, a——'

'I won't listen to such words!' cried Barbara, her eyes in a flame.

'And pray, my dear, how will you prevent my expressing my sincere opinions? You cannot strike me with dumbness because what I say puts you in a rage, can you? I repeat it. You've turned out a shrew and a scold, and I——'

But Wilful had sprung two lengths ahead, under a sudden touch of her heel, and was sending back the sticky soil in showers.

'Oh, that's your game, is it? You vixen!' ground out Dering. He slashed the bay savagely with his cutting whip, and for a moment the two galloped abreast. He laughed exultantly. 'Did you really think you could ride away from me in that style, you mad thing!' he chuckled. 'I'll tell you, then, there's something in the way one rides as well as in one's mount, and you'll find that a poor way of trying to escape me. You saucy vixen, you!'

'Ah, Wilful, off with you, sweetheart!' cried Barbara.

Dering gave a gasp of mingled rage and astonish-
ment, for, gathering his strong legs under him, the
great chestnut swept past and on down the slanting
road, like a streak of fire.  As they flew, Barbara turned
her white face, and, lifting her whip, waved it mock-
ingly.  All the brute was up in Dering.  He desired
only to overtake, to conquer, to crush.  He saw, in the
graceful figure ahead of him, not the woman loved
through happy hours, but an insolent and defiant force
which must be mastered and compelled into the direction which he desired it to take.  The bay's sleek hide
was streaked with weals from his whip, and it pounded
on with all the speed in its power.  Wilful, however,
fleet and light as a deer, steadily increased the distance
between them, until, with an oath, Dering pulled up,
seeing that pursuit was useless.  Then Barbara soothed
Wilful into a walk and waited until Dering came up
with her.  He was too breathless between rage and the
pace at which he had been going to speak for some
time.

Finally he said, with shut teeth :

' You'll be sorry for this.'

'Oh, Jock,' she returned wearily, 'don't threaten. You know that I am not afraid of anything in the world, and that nothing could make me afraid.'

'Upon my soul,' he exclaimed, 'there's something monstrous about you! You're not like a woman. You are like some curious mythological creature. Have you got any heart or blood in you? Heaven help your child! I tremble when I think it's mine, too. It will probably live to curse me and bring disgrace upon my name!'

'You are beside yourself,' said Barbara quietly. 'I forgive you, because I am sure that you don't know what you are saying, but I tell you again that I will not listen. If you go on I shall ride off again.'

'You will, will you? You fury!' he cried, making a lunge at her rein; but she was a perfect horsewoman. Easily avoiding him, she again gave Wilful his head, and, delighted at this game of racing in short heats, he was off and away with a purring snort of pleasure.

When Barbara again allowed Dering to come up with her, they were both silent for some moments. At last she said, in a low voice :

'Jock, don't let us quarrel any more. I am sorry if I have said anything to provoke you, and I know you did not mean the things you said to me just now. Married life is so dreadful if such bitter words are spoken. Somehow one can never quite get over them. They are like ink-spots on a white gown. Either the stain is never completely done away with, or something has to be used which injures the stuff. Either one forgives without forgetting, or forgets because one ceases to care.'

She looked at him earnestly, pleadingly, her heart beating fast, her hand stretched out. For a moment the truth of these words changed Dering's mood. Then his face congealed into its former hardness, and he answered in a cold voice:

'Perhaps you think I don't see your woman's trick of shifting your ground. It was a very clever move, but I am not to be hoodwinked that way. You must have had pretty soft fools to manage before you met me.'

Barbara's face hardened also, and she pressed her lips together in order to keep back a stinging reply.

'I am not the type of husband, let me tell you once for all,' continued Dering, 'who thrives on hen-pecking. Now that I see you care more for that helpless bundle at home than you do for me, I shall retire gracefully. You needn't fear that I will annoy you further. I shall, of course, accept the Lelands' invitation and go West with them. I can't tell when I'll be back. I'll send you my address from Washington.'

He paused as if waiting for her to answer, and she said, in a voice as cold as his own :

'Very well. I hope that you will have a pleasant trip.'

'Thank you,' he replied.

They passed the rest of the ride in silence.

## XXVII.

THE only thought which presented itself clearly to her, in this disturbed seething of her mind, was that she must get away from the house—from everyone—to that deep loneliness of nature which had always seemed to her, in wild moments, like a tranquil hand upon her heart.

She did not ring for Rameses, but took off her habit with nervous haste and drew on her short walking-skirt and mountain-boots. As she stole swiftly and noiselessly along the winding corridors she felt, as she had so often done in a bad dream, as if she were being drawn backward; as if some hand might catch and detain her; as if Dering were about to step before her from some dark closet or turning. At last, however, she was out in the large air of the winter day. Already the sun was trailing after him the languid shadows of his westering course. The ploughed fields showed a soft feathering of young oats, and great clods, smooth from the ploughshare, crumbled like nuggets of burnt gold in the level glare. Clouds, delicate, transparent, rosy - white, meshed the dim azure of the sky. Here and there came a bleak glimmer of snow from some violet shadow. The soft trill - like drip of thawing snow upon dead leaves made a sweet whisper throughout the winter wood. Above, the heavens were hung between the mist of branches like a great blue cobweb. She heard some fox-hounds, far up the mountain-side, swell their deep plaintive notes, and turning into a little path that zigzagged upward among the underbrush, quickened her steps in the direction of their baying.

A chill fragrance from the damp junipers soon enveloped her, and the patches of snow grew thicker and broader. She saw upon this white carpet the marks of birds' feet, the print of little hoofs. It seemed to her, in the exhilaration of climbing, that some baby fawn might have scampered away into the distant mist of soft, gray, leafless stems.   The acorn which he had been nibbling lay there beside the hoof-prints.   Morsels of yet unmelted snow clung here and there to the dark cedar boughs like drowsy white birds.   Even the moist red clay had a clean perfume of its own, and a hare, warily stealing towards a baited trap, paused, quivered up on its haunches, and, display-ing its sleek breast and fine-veined ears, fixed on her its liquid eyes ; then all at once, terrified, alert, drummed quickly with its strong hind-feet, and, whirling, leaped away into the tangled weeds.

Her heart began to beat quickly now, and her breath came fast.   She was on the steepest flank of the moun-tain, and the narrow path which she followed wound far above her head.   But the keenness of her mental suffering seemed a force which impelled her body on-ward.   As long as she forced her supple muscles into energy the tumult in her soul seemed quieted.   She grew so warm that, as she walked, she drew off her jacket and threw it across her shoulder.   The heated blood throbbed stinging through her veins, and the exultation of sheer physical life grew upon her with each powerful movement. Presently the quick panting ceased. She closed her lips and breathed easily; took off her white *beret* and ran her fingers through her damp hair. The air made a cool streak across her forehead. It was like the kiss of some invisible but friendly presence. Already that efficient calm of mountain solitude was upon her. Already the valley, with its troubled life, seemed vague, distant, remote, apart; its purplish mist, like the vapours which arise from weird, untranquil dreams; the harsh note of a distant locomotive, like the cry of some unfortunate, half lapped in the incomplete unconsciousness which begets such visions. She thought of those melodious words which ever sing themselves to a silent music of the mind :

' Come down, O maid, from yonder mountain height,
For love is of the valley, come thou down.'

'No, no!' she said aloud. 'True love is of the heights.' And then she started with that strange self-consciousness which overpowers one at the sound of one's own voice falling upon solitude. She paused, and leaned for a moment against a tree to rest. Her collie, who had rushed ahead, came up and gazed at her, panting. The crisp white of a snow-streak near by suggested thirst, and he dashed his sharp muzzle along its crust and gobbled a mouthful or two, then looked eagerly up at Barbara again, who gave her girlish laugh, and, stooping, gathered a handful, which she ate daintily. Her blood, changed by the vigorous exercise of the last half-hour, was ready to receive new impressions. This plentiful silence pressed against her, charged with myriad suggestions. The soft hand was upon her heart.

In Barbara there was much of that bounteous pagan spirit which first stirred the world to belief in the soul permeating all things. To her each leaf, each transient cloud, each shadow traced in varying light, each fluctuating splendour of the day had its individuality, its message, its conscious being, as of what we call spirit. To her the friendly silence was, at the same time, comprehending. There seemed to rise a courage and consolation to her from the strong, bitter smell of the damp earth. The wind, seizing her roughly by hair and garments, was more sympathetic than the alien presence of another human being. The forward leap of a swollen mountain stream beat sharp and true upon a like chord in her heart—its rush, its turbidness, its savagery, she had felt them all. When a bird alighted near her, unafraid, even ventured to peck at the branch of scarlet berries which she had broken off, from the mere child-wish to have its beauty with her on her lonely walk, she was faint with pleasure at its sweet confiding, and feared to breathe, lest she should frighten it from her. If, by some magic, she could have thrown herself into its being, how quickly she would have mastered its loves, its dreads, its pleasures ! How, as a girl, this desire to be one with the all-spirit had possessed her ! She had longed to be a thousand different women, to pass through a thousand experiences, happy and sorrowful, to exhaust, by a series of brilliant existences, every world in space, to feel all, see all, know all, possess all — laughter, wretchedness, despair, glory, failure, victory, beauty. She had tried to imagine how the growing flowers felt, the trees, the humming-birds swinging in the crape-myrtle bells. How huge everything must have looked to them! How intensely they must have felt! She would have liked to suck the very essence of life, in a few hours of vivid frenzy. As a bird, she would have flown until her wings failed and she had dropped swift and straight into the sea below, or dashed her head against the great glass of some glaring lighthouse.

This old mood caught and shook her to the soul. A blind despair of longing for her dead maidenhood over-rushed her. She put both arms about the huge bole of the tulip-tree against which she leant and pressed her lips to its rough bark. In her heart were some such thoughts as these: 'Dear tree! if I were only a Dryad, and, folded in your fragrant rind, could listen to the stealthy pulsing of the sap through your great boughs, and grow glad with the spring which will make you green again; if, resting so, a part of you as your young leaves will be, I could feel with you the thrill of the midnight storm, the clutching feet of frightened birds, the palpitations of close-scrambling squirrels; in the morning the clash of your ice-coated branches, glittering golden through the fresh sunlight; at sunset to be warmed gloriously and drowned in sheets of flame-colour; to rest, to sleep, to live in you and with you, and then, freeing myself in certain hours of liberty, to range the voiceless woods, unafraid of snow or storm, secure in delicate emotions, incapable of disturbance!'

All this, wildly and chaotically massed, surged through her, as she clung to the great tree, her tears first warming and then chilling her flushed face. While she paused there, however, a gray flag of cloud had been unrolled above. There was a shiver of wind throughout the forest. A drop fell upon her outstretched hand—another, yet another. But suddenly the wind veered and tore an oval space in the steaming air above—a rift of blue sky shone serenely as a gem, widened into placid magnificence, possessed the upper day. That stronger, eager life-joy welled ever higher in Barbara. Her red lips were parted. Her eyes were eager as Robin's, who leaped and circled in front of her like her keen mood made visible.

Now the baying of the hounds rang out again—first near at hand, then growing fainter and fainter in the distance. She reached a primitive fence, made of a rail or two stuffed with underbrush, and in a bound was over, Robin close at her heels. The trees were growing thinner, and dwindled finally into plantations of sassafras, with here and there the glossy green plume of a scrub pine.  All at once she found herself in a steep open field, covered with rustling yellow broom, which came into exquisite contrast with the floating clouds beyond.  Above, on the comb of the hill, was a bristling of purple sassafras-bushes against the white-blue sky, their stems hidden by the rich broom-straw, which grew above her shoulders.  The dim red path wound up and up, and all about was that dry, seething sound, followed by a soft rattle in the limbs of the stunted pear-tree  springing from a pile of stones. Here and there velvety scarlet pyramids of sumac-berries burnt on their blue-gray stems.  The far valley was like a pale-lilac cloth spread smoothly.  It seemed to melt away at last and to become absorbed in space. Above, the small, round, overlapping clouds were like the shells on a broad beach, and they were suggested again by the little ovals of snow clustering in the shadows of the hillside.  A golden robin on a sassafras-

tree, near her foot, turned its head sideways and peered
up at her, half its brilliant speck of eye hidden by the
bluish lower lid. A pregnant and spacious silence
floated on every side. Barbara drew a long breath,
and, sinking on her knees, stretched out her young, vigorous arms, as though yearning over the sorrowful
world which lay spread out beneath her. In those
throbbing moments she realized why Christ had with-
drawn upon mountains to pray. The noble outlines
of the dumb, majestic peaks about her were themselves
like petrified prayers. Here upon this great crest a
purer air came winnowing in, a holier light seemed to
diffuse itself from the near heavens. Here there was
only the soothing acquiescence of nature, the bounteous and unobtrusive peace which hallows the dwell-
ings of humble creatures, whose lives are passed in
such loneliness, and who are content to know the distant valley only as a great chessboard with squares
of amethyst and carnelian glimmering mysteriously
through a lawny haze. She seemed to have left her
anger, her rebellion, her despairing grief all there
under the roof of Rosemary, which she saw with its

clustering out-houses glittering like a handful of pearl-coloured pebbles among its smoke-like trees, far below her. Her heart contracted, as she thought of returning to it. Unfastening her heavy hair, she plunged her fingers into its masses and let the wind streak coolly through it. There was only the golden robin, the sheer air, the rustling broom-field, her dog, to witness this unconventionality. She laughed to feel the strong gusts combing out her loose locks behind her like a gleaming pennon. She felt enveloped by a sweet friendliness of things animate and inanimate, and as though she had grown backward, reaching again her blithe girlhood. Even Valentine was like some quiet hero, of whom she had read in a jewelled book of fairyland — Dering and her child part of an uneasy dream. She was sixteen, as she lay there among the feathery stalks of broom, her hands clasped beneath her head, her hair blowing loose about her. It seemed to her that she was on the prow of a great ship which was plunging onward through billows of golden air.

Then presently she got to her feet, twisted up her hair,

and, calling to Robin, began to climb again, for the summit of the mountain was not yet reached. The path now broadened into a road, which, skirting the edge of a thick wood, brought her finally to another fence. Beyond this lay a cornfield, from which the meadows below looked of a soft gray rose colour. Still farther hung a curtain of bluish mist, and against this mellow background the stripped corn-stalks lifted their tufts of faded orange leaves. The furrows were still striped with snow.

Through this meadow Barbara and Robin went running until they came to a sharp declivity, down which the road plunged boldly, to rise again on a hillside, steeper than any yet, its top outlined by another fence and the gray puffs of leafless apple-boughs. When they had climbed this, however, Barbara, leaning breathless against the lichened rails, looked down into an unfamiliar valley, and saw, like a wall of lapis-lazuli austerely carved against the soft pale air, the vague and spiritual beauty of the Blue Ridge.

A man was ploughing on the hill-crest opposite. The horses moved in patient silhouettes, urged on by his wailing cries. Something glistened on the fence not far from her. She looked at it more closely, and saw that it was a dead black snake trailed limply over the top rail. Some negro had put it there as a sure charm for the long-needed rain.

Barbara smiled sadly and shook her head, as she thought of poor monkeys crucified by the Hill tribes of India for the same purpose as that which had prompted this Virginian darky to kill a snake and hang it on the fence which bore its name.

But now the sky began to pulse with a faint rose hue, the call of nestward birds trembled overhead ; there was that faint, unmistakable stirring through wood and field which is nature's preparation for the calm of night. Barbara wished to see the sunset from the broom-grown hill which overlooked her own well-loved valley. Something in the unfamiliarity of this vast beauty made her sorrowful. She turned and trudged quickly over the slippery snow-clogged roads, until she was once more in the field of broom, with only the great undulating plains between her and the open sea. She called Robin, and, with her arm about him, waited for that puissant change which makes the magic of the sky.

Above spread a lustrous sheet of beryl-coloured air, seen through a filigree of clouds, gray, diaphanous, tinged at their edges with a warm gold. Underneath, a deep-blue mystery of vapour was piled from east to west. as though in imitation of the mountains from which she had just turned away. In this a beamy opening sent forth suddenly shafts of light and revealed what seemed to be an endless waste of molten brass, its tunnelled waves breaking in fiery spume even above the edge of the sombre wall.

The space of tremulous pale green above died into a dim saffron. Little by little the molten brass changed into lead. The glowing door was shut. Upon the level sadness of the far east the full moon balanced like a plaque of silver. A star gleamed here and there with vacillations of green, of red, of orange. Now a white steam rolled upward with the calm moon on its breast. Again came the sensation of being on the prow of a great ship. The ship was the world. It seemed sailing steadfastly through those volumes of cool mist. The darkness began to gather, with its undulations of gloom, of unfamiliar sound, of penetrating odours. The eerie trilling of an owl fell through the thickening air, and once more the baying of the hounds came faintly from the valley.

Suddenly the terror of vast and spacious darkness clutched at Barbara's heart. She started to her feet and gazed about her. The trees no longer seemed friendly, but their dark tracery against the sky was a wizard-writing full of evil. Those surges of wan vapour seemed in her wild thought like a condensation of ghosts, and the owl's cry shivered along her overstrained nerves in a sinister warning. Holding Robin convulsively by the collar, she started down the steep path.

' Ah, my God !' she said aloud after awhile, panting for breath, ' I am so lonely! I have tried so hard ! He will be harsh and stern to me when I come in. I have only my child. Show me my duty to her. I cannot leave her, even if it makes him angry with me for ever. Let me teach her to be a wiser, calmer, happier woman than I have ever been.'

The moon bloomed suddenly into full splendour, and

the fine tracery of the cedar tassels was thrown upon the snow. That convulsive spasm of dread released her, and a strong sense of the beneficence of nature distilled itself again through her whole being. She walked rapidly, but calmly, trying not to think, but to absorb strength for the coming struggle. Once she stopped. It was to lift the rough wooden door of a hare-trap and let scamper the frightened creature within, but she left in its place one of those loose coins which she always carried with her on all her rambles.

Somehow the thought of the hare which she had restored to liberty cheered all her mood. She had learned to regard freedom as so infinite a compensation for most ills, that, to her, even the bondage of a hare seemed not without consequence in the general scheme of existence.

## XXVIII

DURING the next two or three days Fair seemed to be so much better that Barbara was very puzzled as to what course to take in regard to the matter of going West with the Lelands. She felt that Dering would have a right to be angry with her, if, from a vague anxiety, she allowed him to set off alone when Eunice would so gladly take charge of Fair.

The next night, while lying awake in the vain endeavour to decide upon what to do, a sudden thought took possession of her, and, jumping out of bed, she threw on her dressing-gown, lighted a candle, and wrote the following letter to Bishop Cammersell:

' MY DEAR BISHOP,

' You told me so often during your visit to Eunice, last month, that you wished me to come to you in any

trouble, that I am writing to you now for counsel. Indeed, dear Bishop, I am so bewildered and unhappy
that I cannot see clearly, and am utterly confused about
my real duty. My little girl has been seriously ill with
diphtheritic sore-throat, and the doctor tells me that she
is liable to other attacks during all the winter.

'Now, my husband is very anxious for me to go
West with him on a pleasure-party arranged by some
friends, and, of course, I wish to do this if possible,
especially as several things have occurred which may
make it a serious question, and involve much unhap-
piness for us both, in the future, if I am forced to refuse
him. But I cannot bear to leave Fairfax, even in the
charge of Eunice, because I feel that if anything should
happen to her I could never get over it. Besides, I
suppose that a mother always feels that she can do for
her child what no one else in the world can. If, however, you tell me that this is merely a mother's over-
anxiousness, and that the sensible and right thing is
to go with my husband, I will do as you say. I feel
that I am incapable of judging impartially in this matter,
and that Eunice, being herself a very nervous mother,

could not help me.　It is for this that I turn to you,
dear Bishop, for you have had children yourself, and
must often have felt as harassed as I feel now.　I wish
only to be shown my duty.　When I see it I will do it,
no matter what it costs me.　Thanking you beforehand,
dear Bishop, for what I know will be your wise and
helpful answer,

　　　　　　　　' I remain always

　　　　　　　　　　' Yours most sincerely,

　　　　　　　　　　　　' BARBARA DERING.'


For seven days Barbara examined eagerly each post
that came to Rosemary in search of Bishop Cammersell's reply, but in vain.　On the eighth morning she
rode Wilful over to The Poplars and asked Eunice
what she thought of his silence.　They decided that he
could not have received the letter, and Barbara was
forced to rely on her own judgment.

As Fair was again feverish on Monday, she told Dering
finally that she could not go, and on Tuesday he knocked
at her bedroom door and gave her a cool touch on her
cheek for good-bye.　She ran after him.

'Oh, Jock, don't let us part like this! We can never tell what may happen! Won't you say you understand how I feel—that you know I would go with you if I could?'

'I don't perceive any shackles about you, now that I examine you attentively,' said Dering. 'You aren't rooted to the ground, as they say in books, are you?'

He laughed and lighted a cigar. Still the woman in Barbara whispered foreboding, and she clung to his arm.

'Oh, won't you give me a loving kiss, dear?' she pleaded, her eyes wet. 'Dear, you must know how I love you. If anything happened to me, you would suffer so.'

'"Her majesty myself" to the last, eh?' he said.

Stung to the quick, she loosed his arm, and Dering, blowing a mocking kiss from his finger-tips, ran downstairs.

As days went by and still nothing was heard from Bishop Cammersell, Eunice, who happened to be in Ashleigh, called on the Bishop. He was just going out, but took off his hat and cloak and carried her back to his study, where a fire of sea-coal shimmered in an open grate. One of his nine daughters, a slim, fashionably-dressed young woman, with a great deal of flaxen hair and her father's silky blue eyes, came in and brought Eunice a cup of tea, then, with a few pretty words of excuse, left them alone.

' Bishop,' said Eunice, with her usual quiet frankness, going at once to the point, ' I want to ask you about a letter that Barbara Dering wrote you two weeks ago. It was a very important letter, and she looked for your answer with a great deal of anxiety. Did you ever receive it ?'

The Bishop stroked his mildly-retreating chin, and, giving his gentle smile, answered in an explanatory tone :

' Well, you see, my dear child, it is a very delicate and even a dangerous matter to answer such letters. I do not believe in interfering between husband and wife, my child. They have accepted each other for better, for worse. Such questions are always very painful and embarrassing.'

Eunice sat looking at him calmly with her steadfast eyes, but her colour deepened.

' Then you did receive the letter?' was all that she said when the Bishop stopped speaking.

He looked confused and rather uncomfortable, but again smiled benevolently.

' Yes, my dear, I did receive your friend's letter, but I did not think it wise to answer it. A wife should decide such questions for herself. Mr. Dering would have every right to be angry with me if I had meddled in his private affairs.'

Eunice was silent, smoothing and buttoning her little gray *suède* glove. The Bishop continued with restored suavity, being accustomed to take silence for consent :

' You see, my dear child, it is on these impulsive and excitable natures that the discipline of marriage has the most beneficial influence. Your friend will be a much better, wiser, more resigned and Christian woman for being left to settle such questions for herself, with the aid of earnest prayer ; and, pardon me for wounding you, my dear child, but I have been intending to speak to you on this subject ever since my visit to you in the early autumn. I am sure, from careful observation, my dear, that you indulge and subordinate yourself too much to your friend.

True, she is very winning and delightful, but strangely erring and misguided in many ways. Besides, you have your own gifts to cultivate. Many people have told me of your very lovely voice. We should not neglect the talents that a gracious Father has seen fit to bestow upon us, my dear. How sweet it would be if you could train and lead a fine choir in that pretty Gothic church which everyone admires! The music which they now have is painful even to my uncultivated ears. Why not consecrate your beautiful voice to its loving Creator and rejoice the hearts of the congregation? Let your friend rely more upon her own strength—your duty is to yourself, your husband, your children, and your own gifts. Do not spend so much of your precious time with her. Remember that we must each work out our salvation with fear and trembling.'

He paused, his placid lips wreathed by his most engaging smile, his tremulous blue eyes fixed yearningly upon her. But Eunice, her face pale and chill, rose to her feet and stood looking at him, without making any movement to meet his outstretched hands. Then she said slowly, deliberately :

' Bishop, I have only one question to ask you. Do you think that if our Lord had been upon earth, and received such a letter as Barbara wrote you, He would have left it unanswered ?'

The Bishop's rosy cheeks grew rosier, and he smoothed his chin after his manner when slightly puzzled or embarrassed.

' Er—such a letter would scarcely be addressed to our Lord, my dear,' he replied finally.

' Such prayers are often addressed to Him,' said Eunice coldly. ' And we are taught that no prayer remains unanswered, whether as we would have it or otherwise. No matter if your answer had been harsh and uncomprehending, it would have been better than none. You are a Father of our Church, Bishop. Do you think in your inmost heart that you have treated Barbara Dering as a father would treat a cherished daughter ?—as Christ would have treated her ? The reasons that you have given me would be cold-hearted in a layman, how much more in a high-priest of God ! I must bid you good-bye, Bishop. I dare not say to you what is in my heart.'

With a quick movement she left the room, and a few moments later found herself walking rapidly down the broad village street, without knowing in what direction. Eunice's nature was naturally orthodox and easily guided, but the dialogue in which she had just taken part caused in her a strong reaction. She recalled the words which speak of there being One only Mediator between God and man, the man Christ Jesus, and regretted, in her sudden revulsion of ideas, that it was considered necessary to approach Him through the medium of bishops, priests, and deacons. How much sweeter it was to speak to Him directly, looking up into the deep blue of the sky! How much more solemn sounded the still, small voice now whispering in her heart than the unctuous tones of Bishop Cammersell! How much easier it was to approach Him in spirit, than bodily through the conventional means of weekly church-going! She walked on faster and faster, until at last arrested by the bright face of a little girl, who was leaning against a gate arranging her school books more satisfactorily under her arm.

'Who lives here, dear?' asked Eunice, more for

want of something to say than from any real desire to know.

' Oh, don't you know ?' exclaimed the child, starting away from the gate and looking frightened. ' I thought ev'ybody in Ashleigh knew that! It's the black-eyed minister's house !'

This mysterious announcement only made Eunice laugh gently. The child looked up at her, also smiling.

' And who is the black-eyed minister ?'

' Oh, he's a good man, they say, but dreadful cross an' hard. He thinks God's always mad with ev'ybody. An' his church is so bare an' cold all the old ladies get rheumatism, but they go, 'cause when folks *do* love the black-eyed minister they love him real hard. But mother 'n' me we love Bishop Cammersell. He's jes' like the Lord Jesus in the picture, an' his smile is jes' lovely. An' when he says, " Suffer the little children to come unto Me," after Sunday-school, all the gyrls cry. An' one day he said that about a " cup of cold water in the name of the Lord " when I took him a gourdful from our spring, an' I couldn't help cryin'

myself. Ev'ybody's jes' wild 'bout him. An', oh, he's
got such beautiful white curls, an' his daughters do
dress so stylish ! Mother says they get their clothes
from New York. An' he's always preachin' 'bout
heaven ; but the black-eyed minister *he* preaches most
'bout hell.'

She stopped, out of breath, her chubby face glowing,
the red tape which fastened her slate-pencil to her slate
wrapped so tightly about her forefinger that the flesh between its cross-work was of a yellow-white.

A sudden idea took possession of Eunice. Kissing her
informant, much to that small creature's surprise, she
opened the gate and went up the narrow brick walk to
the black-eyed minister's house.

It was a large stuccoed building, with a square porch
supported on four brick piles. Over one end of this
porch a bare honeysuckle - vine swayed about in the
winter air. Two green tubs, on either side of the
wooden steps, held stunted cactus plants. She could see
behind the shining window-panes dark-red curtains
parted as primly as the hair in an old-fashioned portrait.
There was no door-bell or knocker, so, opening the green

Venetian blinds which protected the front-door, she rapped against its panels with the handle of her umbrella. A round-faced coloured girl in a checked blue cotton gown and a big white cap answered the knock, and said her master was at home.

Eunice sat down on a horsehair sofa in the sitting-room and looked about her. The whitewashed walls bore the marks of the brush, and there were family photographs in oval mahogany frames hung at regular distances over the mantelpiece. Three chairs, also covered with black horsehair, were ranged against the walls. There was a marble-topped table, on which rested a handsome old edition of 'Pilgrim's Progress,' a large Bible bound in calf, and a calendar set in ebony. A rectangular bronze clock ticked hoarsely in the centre of the mantelshelf, and on either side of it was a tall bronze candlestick, from which rose a tallow candle.

The room was very cold, and Eunice did not unfasten her jacket, but sat with her hands in her muff, trying to imagine the black-eyed minister's outward appearance by studying the photographs in the mahogany frames.

Suddenly the door opened, and an immense man appeared on the threshold, fixing on her his sunken but piercing eyes.  On his gaunt frame hung a suit of rusty black, his dark hair, short and straggling, showed a gray thread here and there.  His clean-shaven face was crossed by haggard lines.  His lips were but a firm line above his massive chin.  The contrast of his appearance to that of Bishop Cammersell was as striking as though a pennon of black crape were to be set floating from an iron stanchion against a rosy apple-tree.  He coughed before speaking, and then said :

' My servant did not mention your name, madam.'

' I am  Eunice Bransby—Mrs. Godfrey Bransby,' said Eunice, a little nervously.  ' I  do not  even know your name, sir.   I have a friend who is in great need of advice, and  I  was  told that a minister lived here.   I hope that you won't think I took a liberty.'

He made no direct answer to this appeal, but said, in his bell-like voice :

' My  name  is  George  Macfarlane, and  I  am an Episcopal minister.  Tell me to what denomination you belong, madam.'

'I am an Episcopalian,' replied Eunice shyly, beginning to understand why people preferred dapper Bishop
Cammersell to this iron-visaged priest.

His face relaxed somewhat, and he said :

'Come to my study. We can speak more privately
there, and I will have a fire lighted.'

Eunice followed him over the worn oil-cloth of the
narrow hall, and, opening a door to the left, he showed
her into his study, then called the negro girl, who lighted
two or three shavings of pine-wood under a lump of
coal and left them to their fate, without the aid of a
blower.

The contrast between the Bishop's study and that of
Mr. Macfarlane was as complete as that of their per-
sonalities. The former room, thickly curtained and
carpeted, had walls hung in embossed leather, a luxurious
carved writing-table, lounging chairs deeply cushioned,
sofas, footstools, bookcases lined with every volume
that could edify or instruct an Episcopal prelate's mind.
Here there were several stiff-backed wooden seats, an
uncushioned arm-chair covered with carpeting, dark-
green shades on rollers, an old oak table, and a pine

bookcase not more than half filled with volumes, whose dingy covers showed that they had been long in their owner's possession.   Over the mantelpiece hung a map of the Holy Land, and resting against the wall, just beneath it, was a crayon drawing of an old lady, who looked like Mr. Macfarlane, in a widow's dress and cap.

Eunice could not help smiling, as she glanced up at it, but, seeing that he regarded her gravely, reassumed a serious expression.

'Now, madam,' he said, placing one of the wooden chairs for her and taking another himself.  'If you will tell me your friend's trouble I will try to advise her; but first I should like to know why she did not come herself.   Is she ill?'

'She does not know that I intended seeing anyone for her to-day,' answered Eunice; 'but she wrote to—to another minister, who never answered her letter.'

'Did he receive it?' said Mr. Macfarlane.

'Yes.'

'And was it a letter asking for advice?'

' Yes.'

' A respectful letter ?'

' It was a noble, simple, touching letter, sir,' said Eunice earnestly. ' I read it before my friend posted it. In it she asked as humbly as a child to be shown her duty. She said that when she knew what it was she would do it, no matter at what cost to herself.'

' And you are sure that it was received ?'

' Perfectly sure. I went myself to see the person to whom it was written, and the only reasons he gave for not answering it were that it was a very delicate and dangerous matter to interfere between husband and wife, and that, had he done so, my friend's husband would have had just cause to be angry with him. He also said that wives ought to know how to decide such questions for themselves.'

Mr. Macfarlane's face grew sterner and sterner, but when she finished speaking, all that he said was :

' And now tell me the cause of your friend's trouble.'

Eunice told him in as few words as possible, and when she finished he looked at her with eyes softened by a great kindliness.

'You may tell your friend for me,' he then said, 'that I am glad in these days of careless motherhood to hear of a young woman who, in spite of such painful obstacles, sees her duty so clearly and performs it so bravely. It would indeed be better for a mother to have a millstone hanged about her neck and to be drowned in the depths of the sea than to offend a little one whom God has given into her keeping, body and soul. If your friend is in further perplexity of any sort, I hope that she will come to me. At least I will give her my honest counsel, without thinking of the unpleasant consequences which it may bring upon myself. As for you, madam, your love for your friend is very beautiful, and the feeling which exists between you is a holy and blessed thing which you cannot prize too highly or thank God for too earnestly. I hope that this chance meeting may grow into a fuller acquaintance, madam, and I assure you again of my hearty approval of your friend's conduct.'

Eunice thanked him again and again, and when they parted at the door he took her hands in his, and said, with deep gentleness :

'I may have seemed cold to you, my child. My manner has always been a source of regret to me; but you have my blessing. I thank God that I have been of service to you.'

Eunice looked up into the dark eyes with a sensation of tears behind her own. As she went down the rickety wooden steps she had lost all sense of his hardness, and could readily believe that ' when folks did love the black-eyed minister they loved him real hard.'

## XXIX

THREE weeks passed before Barbara got a letter from Dering, although she had written to him very regularly. His words were saltless, largely scrawled, and touched only on practical matters. Barbara refolded the cold, thick sheets and put them back into their envelope with a dry sensation at heart and eyes. She had not yet reached what Carlyle calls ' the centre of indifference,' although she was beginning to feel that its arid calm, as of the central point in a cyclone, might be a safe retreat from the turbulences of her present life.

After a few moments spent quietly at one of the open windows, she ordered Wilful and started upon a long ride.

It was now the middle of April, the air mild as a fairy's breath, the pear-trees one flutter of white blossom, the peach-trees frailly rosy, the young leaf-buds on the maples and poplars making a dim green dust between her and the distant horizon. Yellow crocus-tips were just breaking the black garden mould here and there, and violets crowded damp and pungent under their matted leaves. On the greening hillsides the sheep moved lazily, their dull-pink wool, tinted by the red soil, melting into the general harmony about them. The incessant bleating of the lambs was punctuated by the sharp ' tink-tink ' which came from the bell-wether's neck. A hundred different bird-notes thrilled the fluctuant air. The singers whirred their gay wings close to Barbara's cheek, swung head down as though tipsy with sunshine among the honeyed white of the pear-trees, alighted in Wilful's haughty way and were off again before he could send a purring breath of inquiry through his dilated nostrils. Butterflies clear as amber and smoother than satin tilted past on the placid breeze. The spongy soil gave forth a delightful per-fume, as of the quintessence of spring. The noise of distant brooks came tremulously to the ear. Under-foot was a dark tangle of periwinkle, in which, here and there, a pale-blue flower-star glimmered or a toad-stool perked its fat, white stem, on which sat the round umbrella-like top, as daintily browned as a well-made *meringue*. In this part of the lawn white pines grew thickly, and the earth was dank and rich. Wild vines covered the tree-stems and rioted along the ground, in friendly interlacings with the glistening periwinkle trails. Wild strawberries were here in bloom, and here in the scraggy branches of lopped cedars which had died from age one could see the soft round of nests and the glint of faintly-coloured eggs.

When Wilful had jumped the octagon, moss-crusted rails of the old fence which girdled the grounds, they broke at once from the twilight of thick evergreens into the full splendour of the day. There was a wash of lucent gold from east to west.

A veil of transparent yet throbbing glory seemed lowered between Barbara's eyes and the wide valley about her. Beyond was the pale-green shimmer of young oats, undulations of deep-red soil breaking the tender monotony, tufty woods, their shadows softened by a vapoury azure, thin crests of tall stone-pines glowing dark and bright as

splendid emeralds. The red-bud trees made globes of
dusky colour far away, symmetrical and fragile-looking
as though they had been dandelion-balls dyed crimson.
The sky was a hood of harebell-tinted silk trimmed lace-
like with pale clouds.

Barbara rode on and on, breathing deep of the generous
air, and feeling with a healthful pleasure the elastic
movements of her horse. She was in perfect accord
with the fertile beauty of the day and season, and her
own glowing loveliness struck no note of contrast, but
was rather an accentuation of the vivid wonders about
her.

She came finally to a branching road which ran south-
ward through a belt of timber towards what was called
‘the flat woods.’ And while she hesitated, Wilful, as
though deciding for her, wheeled suddenly and began to
gallop along this level way. At first she frowned and
tried to turn him, but, with a sudden change of mood,
urged him on; and so they galloped for a long while
through the spring forest, which was softly green overhead and fragrant with the breath of wild azaleas. At
length the railway was crossed, and they were well on

their way to the different country which lay beyond the flat woods.

Between Barbara's brows was the little crease which, with her, always meant determination. After they had gone about eight miles she drew up beside a broad willow-edged stream and let Wilful pick his way carefully down the bank and thrust his muzzle deep into the lazy water.

As he drank, a little flotilla of white geese sailed gently up across the silver reflections of the willows, out-dazzling the radiant clouds above. Their deep-orange bills seemed almost like flames darting from their sleek heads, and on this fiery yellow the small nostrils looked like specks of jet. A bird shook the willow-branch near her with its swift alighting and began its cheery call. As a child, Barbara had fancied that it said, ' We greet you! We greet you! We greet you! Now! Now! Now! Now!'

She looked up in time to see its glistening breast and delicate claws before it flew off, glittering like a bit of spun glass in the fresh glare, then, Wilful having sighed deeply, in token that he was content and ready to start, they went on along the now level roads.

A half-hour more of trotting and cantering, varied by a steady walk now and then, brought them to a huge old gate of wrought iron, swung between granite posts, on the balls of which clung falcons with their wings spread. A tumble-down stone wall, held from utter dilapidation in many places by the strong bands of the Virginia creeper, ran from this gate to right and left until hidden by hedges of mock-orange. Barbara opened the heavy gate with her riding-crop as though accustomed to its eccentricities, for she was careful to hold the handle of her whip against it until Wilful was well through, when it clanged to again as though with a spring.

The road was no longer red, but of a gray-white, and wound along between gently-curving fields, downy with young grass and sometimes dignified by an immense oak, on whose gnarled branches the tender leaves had an in-appropriate and frivolous look, sometimes varied by the tall streak of a Lombardy poplar like a Titanic exclama-tion point against the blond sky. A long avenue of Norway spruces made a dark tunnel through the bril-liant wall of the day, and under these Barbara guided Wilful.

These trees were very old and grew in fantastic shap
One was like a vast lyre, another was twisted into a h· ·
S, another resembled the zigzag of the conventio· ·.
thunderbolts grasped by Zeus in a child's mytholo  ·
Their young cones, oozing with sap, hung brightly gre·
among the sombre tassels.   Wilful's hoofs struck nois ·
lessly upon the matting of brown tags, or crunched up· ·
the dry resin-tipped cones of last year's growth.  A warn ·
thrilling odour enfolded her, and through the openin  ·
in the dark boughs little slits of sunlit grass beyo·  ·
shone with a jewelled brightness.                      ·

At the end of this avenue there was a gate, whic·
opened upon a field of wheat, and in the centre of thi·
field a white oblong gleamed through a railing c
iron.

When Barbara reached the gate she slipped down,
tied Wilful to one of its posts, and, passing through
closed it as gently as though she were entering the
room of a sleeping child.  With her habit gathered
under one arm, and her eyes bent gravely on the narrow
path, she walked on towards the white stone.  A young
larch-tree grew near the iron railing, and as she reached

it she saw that someone was standing on the other side, for a white gown showed through the fringe of foliage. This figure was slight and small, and leaned with one cheek against the hand which grasped the rusty iron above its head. The other hand held a basket of white and blue violets. Beyond was a foam of young pear-trees—the grass of the enclosure was freaked with their blown petals.

'Kitty?' said Barbara, whispering, and with a certain questioning inflection as though doubtful of her welcome.

The girl turned with a violent start, her face pale, her eyes wide. They looked at each other a moment in silence. Then Barbara made an impetuous movement, and caught the other to her breast, kissing her, at the same time, on the cheeks, hair, and forehead.

'Forgive me, Kitty,' she said at last. 'You used to love me.'

'I have never stopped loving you,' murmured the girl faintly. She was trembling, and her basket of violets lay overturned at her feet. 'But why—why——' She broke off and stood devouring Barbara's face with her large eyes, which, although of a soft blue, were strangely like Dering's.

'Why have you come here?' she went on abruptly. 'Are you happy?'

'No, dear,' said Barbara quietly. 'But I thought you were in Normandy still at school, Kitty. I thought no one was here but the old servants.'

'No. I came last week. Aunt Miriam is with me.' Then she added timidly: 'I will go away, Barbara, and—and come back—afterwards, if you wish.'

'Thank you, dear Kitty,' answered Barbara, in the same still voice. 'That will be very sweet of you.'

'And the violets—I should love you to have them,' suggested Kitty shyly.

But Barbara shook her head.

'No, dear, that is your own offering. Those lovely pear-blossoms are all that I could wish. But thank you, darling—thank you, darling Kitty.'

The girl threw herself upon Barbara's breast with a sudden movement.

'Oh, Barbara,' she cried, 'you love him best! You love him best! I have known it always. I was only a little thing, but I knew you couldn't love another time as you loved him. Tell me it's true, Barbara! Tell me! tell me !'

' It's true, sweetheart,' said Barbara, her lips white.

' Oh, thank God !' cried the girl. 'Thank God ! But how sad ! I am very cruel. You must be so miserable, Barbara.'

' Not always,' answered Barbara gently. ' There are different ways of loving, dear child.'

'And you love this one a different way?' asked Kitty, a tinge of jealousy sharpening her voice.

' Yes, dear.'

' You do love him, then ! Is he good to you ?'

' He loves me as he has never loved anyone else.'

'As you loved Val ?'

' No ; men don't love like that.'

' Val loved you like that. More than that !' cried the girl, with sudden fierceness. ' *He* would never have married again. I've heard him say so.'

Barbara was silent, her lips still pale.

' Oh, forgive me !' cried Kitty, with a gush of tears. 'I have never judged you, Barbara. I—I know how

much he was like Val.   I shall always love you.   I shall
never say anything to hurt you again.'

Barbara tried to smile in sign of forgiveness, but
her parted lips only trembled, and two large tears ran
slowly from her lowered eyelids.   Kitty kissed them
away, with passionate murmurs of self-reproach, and
whispered :

' I'll leave you now, darling.   Stay as long as you wish.
I'll keep everyone away.'

Barbara nodded, and after one more straining embrace
Kitty turned and ran swiftly along the winding path which
led to the avenue of spruce-trees.

When she was out of sight Barbara gathered an armful
of the white pear-bloom, and, entering the enclosure, went
and knelt beside the white stone.   She had taken off her
riding-hat, and the April sunshine lighted her hair.
After a little while she bent and kissed the grass which
covered Valentine's grave ; then, turning, pressed her
lips to the carved letters of his name.   She kept them
there so long that the cold marble grew warm beneath
her touch.   With one hand she smoothed the long grass
as though it had been the coverlet of her child.   An

irrepressible anguish mingled with a solemn joy rose through her veins until her submerged heart felt as though it must suffocate.

'My darling! my darling! my darling!' she said over and over. 'My own! my very own! My first love! my kind love! my best love!'

Her tears now fell so fast that her cheeks were wet, as though bathed in rain. There was no sobbing—only the continual gush, as though from the very fountain of her soul. It seemed to her that she knelt there, in that ecstasy of exquisite pain and tenderness, for a long while. Then, as though remembering a forgotten duty, she began to lay the pear-blossoms very gently upon the mound beside which she knelt, almost as though she feared to waken someone. Afterwards she put her arm about the stone, and, leaning her cheek against it, was motionless again. She felt no need of explaining anything, even to her own heart. She had made a sorrowful mistake, but it was only sorrowful, not wilful, and she felt that her 'kind love' would understand, as he had always done. The love that she gave him, so passionately ethereal in its lastingness, immortalized him until he seemed to her a very presence—as real as the sunlight about her, although as intangible. She had needed the terrible experience of her second marriage to learn the lesson of real love—that love which is the result of perfect companionship, of mutual reverence, of soul-accord as fine and perfect as that of two instruments keyed to the same pitch, which is as indescribable as perfume, as ineffable as the music heard in dreams; to which passion bears the relation of his sceptre to a king, its colour to a flame; which is neither entirely tenderness nor entirely fire, but that royal blending of the two which means completeness; a feeling in which nature becomes divine and divinity natural; which gives wings to the heart, and hallows, by its supreme instinct, every subtlest detail of human life. This love, unknowing, she had given to Valentine—still gave it to him, chastened and intensified by the anguish she had suffered since his death. But she had also learned to put aside all longing for supreme happiness in her present life. To be supremely strong for the happiness of others was now her heart's desire. In spite of all the pessimism and scepticism of the age there was in her a wholesome fervour

of belief in the final working together of all things for
good, an unconquerable voice which spoke lowly in the
silence of her soul, and which said, 'God is in me and I
in Him.' She had determined to put from her all regrets
which might weaken her power for good in the world
about her. Her love for Valentine must pass from an
unutterable sorrow to a mighty consolation—an upholding
proof of the possibility of idealness in human love. That
she was capable of an emotion so pure, so entirely apart
from the material, gave her a sense of worthiness at once
refreshing and soothing. She honoured her nature,
which was at the same time so loyal, so courageous, and
so wise, for she knew that these quiet hours beside the
grave of her first love separated her life into two parts.
For the last time she yielded herself to these sorrowful
sweet memories. For the last time she gave up her soul
to him. When she turned from that quiet place it would
be to take up her life as it was and to bear it unflinchingly
until the end.

She knew that in a different way, as she had said to
Kitty, she loved Dering, and as she sat there with her
cheek against the stone, she was filled with a profound

determination to make him happy, to help him to develop what was highest in his nature, to win him utterly by her unfailing sympathy and patience.

The air was cooling. A level glimmer drowsed over the green reaches about her. Once more she pressed her lips to the cold marble, clasping it about with her warm arms, as though it had been a living thing and could respond to her passion of renunciation, of farewell, of forgetfulness. Her thick hair, so easy to uncoil, fell down upon its austere whiteness—the hair that he had loved! For the first time she sobbed heart-brokenly.

# XXX.

It was not until the first week of May that Barbara received from Dering any definite account of his plans. She then learned, to her intense surprise, that he had sailed for Japan with another friend, whom he had met in San Francisco, and that the Lelands had already returned to Washington.

A sword-pang went through Barbara's heart. Was she, then, to lose even the compensation of his love? Must she bear her life without the mere comfort of feeling that she bore it for one who loved her, no matter how harshly? She was bewildered, and sat looking at the letter in her hand, and saying, 'God help me! God help me!' in a dulled voice. There was no higher human power to whom she felt like turning for advice. At the thought of Bishop Cammersell her strong lip curled. Mr. Macfarlane was a high-minded but conventional parson, whose ideas of marriage were probably comprised in St. Paul's pithy saying, 'Wives, submit yourselves unto your own husbands, as unto the Lord.' Several hundred years divided her from the people who lived about her—from their creeds and customs. Still, she felt that she must make every effort to keep her husband from drifting wilfully or unconsciously into a life of hard isolation. She went and knelt down by Fair, who was brandishing her pretty legs and tugging at the toes of her gaily-coloured socks, making little clucking sounds of replete pleasure the while.

'Poor baby! what have *you* got to suffer?' she said bitterly.

Fair gave a gurgling laugh for reply, and showed her pink gums with a supreme lack of vanity. Her great eyes, feathered with long lashes, glared brilliantly up into Barbara's face.

'My eyebrows, my hair, my forehead—his eyes and mouth,' she murmured on. 'What is in store for you? Will you suffer most or make others suffer? As you're a woman-child, poor mite, I suppose it is you who'll have the sharpest pangs.'

'A-glee! A-glee! A-glee!' was Fair's response, blotting out her mother's nose and mouth with a down-soft palm.

Barbara kissed it as it clutched at her lips, then, taking it in her own, played with the fingers, so like pale honeysuckle-buds.

'Oh, you pretty one!' she went on presently, tears in her wistful eyes. 'Perhaps by another cradle, at this very minute, another mother, as unhappy as I am, is wondering over the future of the atom who is to darken all your life. Poor babykin! Poor, pretty babykin! I feel half guilty when I look at you. But, oh! if I have learned any wisdom through my own pain, I will try to save you from such tortures—if you will be saved!'

She smiled sadly, sceptically, leaning her head against the railing of the white crib. Fair plunged her released fingers into the heavy coils of hair and jerked them with fierce delight.

'Oh, you cruel little thing!' cried Barbara, starting up, tears of pain succeeding the tears of tenderness. 'Are you beginning to hurt me already?'

'A-glee! A-glee!' bubbled Fair imperturbably, once more attacking the loose toes of her socks, and taking no further notice of her mother.

Barbara went over to the window and stood looking out at the lawn, which was dusted with buttercups.

'How idiotic of me to be hurt by that little creature! And yet I am hurt. I must be more stoical—I will be. I cannot live in this way. Now I will be practical, and go for a long ride. Ramie dear, order Wilful; and, if you would like to, you shall go with me. You can ride the brown mare.'

Rameses, who was a fervent horsewoman, was in an ecstasy of delight. When they started off, she galloped behind her mistress until Barbara turned, with a smile, and beckoned her to her side.

'Now, Ramie dear,' she said, 'I'm a girl again, and so are you, and we are going to talk like sisters. Isn't it a perfect day? Look at those clouds over there with that curious round hole in them. The sunlight streams through like the spokes of a wheel, doesn't it? Why, how strange! how lovely! There's a little rainbow on one side. Look!'

'Dat's what de coloured folks calls a sun-dawg,' answered Rameses.

'And what does it mean?' said Barbara.

'Hit means bad weather.'

'I never saw it before, did you?'

'Oh, yease'm; an' hit always mean *bad* weather— dat sun-dawg mean *bad* weather—he so *beeg*.'

'Well, here's a good piece of road. Let's gallop,' broke in Barbara, with a sigh.

When they pulled up again, she said abruptly :

'Ramie, are you glad or sorry that slavery's over?'

'Why, Miss Barb'ra?'

'Because I'm glad. Those dreadful stories you tell me! I couldn't have borne it. It would have made me so miserable. And yet, when the slaves were happy, they were very happy, weren't they?'

'Some wuz in heaven an' some in hell. Dat wuz de wust of hit,' said Rameses slowly.

'But you?' said Barbara.

'Me? Lor'! Ole miss jes' rottened *me* wid goodness. But shuh! talk 'bout slav'ry, Miss Barb'ra, I'se been a slave an' I'se seen slaves an' I *knows*, an' dis slav'ry uv marriage is de wussest slav'ry in life! Ef I could git free onct, I'd run, ef anybordy call de *name* " man." '

Barbara laughed outright. Then she held out her hand affectionately, and Martha Ellen placed in it her slim brown fingers.

' Are you so unhappy, dear?' said Barbara gently.

' Gawd, *He* knows I'se mizzabul,' answered the other, her great eyes brimming over. ' I'se ben so true an' kine tuh Tobit, Miss Barb'ra. But shuh! mens ain' got de sense dey bawn wid, nohow. Dat critter Tobit run arter, she jes' ez black an' bony ez a griddle!'

Here Martha Ellen's unfailing sense of humour made her show her pretty teeth.

' He isn't worth your little finger,' cried Barbara hotly. ' How can you bear it, Ramie?'

' Wommens *has* tuh bear things, somehow, Miss Barb'ra,' said the other concisely. ' Dat's how I bears hit.'

Barbara was silent for a long while. When she looked about her again, she saw that a great cap of clouds was settling over the fields.

' Hit's dat ole sun-dawg,' said Rameses.

' And my saddle's turning,' replied Barbara. She slipped down and began to investigate, while Martha Ellen held Wilful's bridle. ' Good heavens! the girth's broken. What a bore !'

' An' dat's a *bad* storm comin' up,' said the other ominously. ' You git up on my hawse, Miss Barb'ra an' I'll walk an' lead Wilfur.'

As they were standing there a rattling of wheels came nearer, and Barbara saw that it was Bransby driving alone in the children's buckboard. He stopped to ask if he could help them.

' I don't know,' said Barbara, rather vaguely. ' There's going to be a storm, I think, and my horse is afraid of lightning. I wouldn't mind that, though, but the girth is broken, and I haven't a surcingle.'

' I'll tell you what, Miss Barb'ra,' ventured Rameses. ' Ef Mr. Bransby 'll take you up, I'll lead de hawses tuh Susan Flemin's, over in dat field dere, an' you kin sen' Tobit fur 'em when de stawm's over.'

' Yes, do let me drive you home, Mrs. Dering,' said Bransby, with an attempt at cordiality.

The clouds were now black and veined with such vivid

lightning that Barbara consented, and got into the buck-board. Bransby had no carriage-rugs with him, and Barbara's short, scant habit displayed fully her arched feet in their russet-leather riding-boots.

She smiled a little wickedly as she braced them comfort-ably against the dash-board, remembering how very long poor Eunice was compelled to wear her habit-skirts, and thinking of the wide, old-fashioned trousers which she strapped under her walking-boots. Even this was a con-cession over which Bransby had winced.

As they drove, he so prim and erect, with his neat little hands manipulating whip and reins as daintily as though he had been knitting, the spirit of mischief rose in Barbara, until presently she actually crossed one knee over the other with an air of serene unconscious-ness. She saw Bransby's lips tighten and his brows begin to pleat.

' How fortunate that you came along when you did !' she then said, in her sweetest voice. ' And what a——' She cast about in her mind for Dering's more sporting expressions. ' What a rattling good " gee " you've got there !' she ended glibly.

'Yes, it's an excellent animal,' replied Bransby austerely.

'Rather light of bone, isn't she?' asked Barbara, with a knowing air.

'Of course she is not perfect,' said Bransby.

'Jolly good quarters, though!' she went on calmly. 'Fine barrel! Have you named her yet?'

'No; we are discussing the matter now.'

'Good gracious!' said Barbara, with elaborate innocence. 'Discussing it! Why, there's only one name possible for her!'

'Indeed! And that?' inquired Bransby stiffly.

'"Ballet-girl," of course!'

'"Ballet-girl"? But why, if I may ask?'

'Why, on account of those long stockings. It's the only name, really—and so original.'

'Er—entirely original,' admitted Bransby, with tartness. 'But—er—er—I prefer short names for a horse.'

'Why, call her "Socks," then,' suggested Barbara. 'That's short enough, isn't it?'

'I think I shall let Eunice name her,' he replied.

Barbara, who had been searching for her handkerchief during this conversation, discovered an old cigarette-case of Dering's in one of the pockets of her covert-coat. Her eyes gleamed, but she drew it forth demurely and began examining its contents with an air of intense interest.

'Pshaw!' she exclaimed at last, in a tone of disgust. 'They're all broken! What a shame!'

Bransby could not restrain himself any longer.

'Excuse me, Mrs. Dering,' he said in a withheld sort of tone, 'but as your friend's husband, as a Virginian, I —I must really advise you not to smoke on the public road.'

Barbara, who would as soon have thought of such a thing as of laying Fair on hot coals to secure her immortality, looked up with guileless eyes, and said :

'But why?'

'I do not think your neighbours would understand it. You would be very harshly judged.'

'Oh, I am that now,' she returned easily. 'Having one's neighbours misjudge one is like breaking a pair of boots. Just at first it pinches a little, but that's soon over. However, I won't vex you by smoking.'

' I am extremely indebted to you,' said Bransby.

Barbara took in his whole attitude of controlled disgust from the corner of her eyes, and was as malevolently delighted as a child who has played some naughty prank on an unloved elder. Her fertile mind began to devise new schemes for teasing him. A sudden inspiration made her whistle softly. This accomplishment she possessed in a rare degree, and an impassioned aria from ' Faust ' now fell flutily from her pursed lips. She broke off suddenly, wishing to vary his torture as much as possible, and exclaimed :

' Patti is to be in Washington next week, and " Faust " is the first opera in which she sings. Couldn't we make up a party and go to hear her ? Eunice would enjoy it so heartily.'

' I—er—that is—we never go to the opera,' said the uncomfortable Bransby.

' Not go to the opera !' And again she turned to him with that maddening ' But why ?'

' I disapprove of emotional music.'

'You disapprove of Gounod's music?'

'Yes, and of "Faust" particularly. It is an immoral story, and the music is in a high degree immoral.'

'Oh, you are a disciple of Tolstoi!'

'I agree with him in his views regarding such music, assuredly.'

'But what is there in the music of "Faust" that strikes you as immoral?'

'It is too intense—too—er—er—unnatural. The men and women of to-day do not indulge in such overstrained emotions.'

'But they must, if this music rouses such terribly dangerous sensations in them.'

She saw his face turn a dull red in the gathering twilight.

'It is useless for us to discuss such matters, Mrs. Dering. Our views are entirely opposed.'

'Indeed they are!' breathed Barbara fervently.

Then she began again:

'So you believe that virtue consists in an absence of emotion.'

'I did not say that,' replied Bransby uneasily.

'No, but you implied it. Now I, for my part, think that the more we feel the greater we are, and I have some very good authorities to back me up in this opinion. Gibbon, Mommsen, and Ruskin all agree that genius cannot exist without passion. Life is glorious, and those who feel most live most intensely. To me poor Gretchen's story is one of the tenderest and most touching ever written.'

' Indeed !' said Bransby, with thinned lips.

'I see that it disgusts you. If one of your daughters happened to share the fate of poor Olivia Primrose, you would not act as the old vicar did, would you ?'

' Mrs. Dering, such allusions are intolerable !'

'I beg your pardon. I was simply stating an imaginary case. But it is really a pity for me to make you dislike me more than you do already, because Eunice is so dear to me.'

' Dislike you ?' stammered Bransby.

'Yes—hate me almost. I really think you have indulged in an "intense emotion" there, Mr. Bransby, and I have been fanning it into a still more fervid glow during the last half-hour! What a pity! I love Eunice more than any woman in the world, and her husband dislikes me in proportion.'

'I—I scarcely know you,' murmured the wretched Bransby.

'No; it is instinctive,' said Barbara philosophically. 'But perhaps'—she lifted her eyes to his face—'perhaps we might detest each other less if we knew each other better.'

'So you confess that you do not like me, either!' exclaimed Bransby, catching at this straw.

'Why, you must have known that all along,' said Barbara with calmness. 'Whatever my faults may be, I am not a hypocrite.'

'You think me a hypocrite, I dare say,' returned Bransby.

'No; I think you narrow, and—but what is the use? I shall only make you hate me more.'

'But I wish to know. Please oblige me by finishing your sentence,' said Bransby, with an actual touch of eagerness. 'What is it that you think me, besides narrow?'

'Well, cold-blooded,' said Barbara; 'but you admire cold-bloodedness, so why should you be vexed?'

There was, in fact, no logical reason why Bransby should feel the intense indignation which overwhelmed him at these words. He did not speak for some moments. Black clouds now draped three parts of the sky, and only a faint crocus-coloured light quivered along the north-east. A wild flag of wind was shaken through the air, and a low noise of thunder rolled heavily overhead. Some birds streamed twittering from a tree close by.

'What a storm it is going to be!' exclaimed Barbara, looking about her. 'I don't think we can reach Rosemary in time. The Poplars is nearer.'

A blare of thunder shook the darkening air. Again the birds shrieked and circled, and the mare began to snort nervously and twitch her ears.

'Is she lightning-shy?' asked Barbara.

'I don't know,' answered Bransby, who was rather pale. 'I have only had her a week. But pray don't be alarmed.'

'Oh, don't bother,' she said cheerfully. 'I was never afraid of horses, or lightning either. Besides, one wouldn't get much of a fall from this trap.'

Bransby gave her an admiring glance, in spite of himself. Her attitude was one of such calm ease and self-confidence, as she sat leaning back, one foot braced in front of her, her arms lightly folded. She was not pale. On the contrary, her colour had deepened richly in the strong wind. Her serene eyes were bent upon the ever-narrowing band of yellow glare before them. She looked as composed as a young goddess who had ordered a big thunder-storm for her amusement and was watching its progress from some safe shelter.

'I'm afraid you will be thoroughly drenched,' he said at last. 'I've no rugs with me, and I felt a drop on my cheek just then.'

'That's nothing,' she rejoined gaily. 'I'm neither rheumatic nor consumptive, or, as my old mammy used to put it, I'm not made of salt or sugar, and won't melt. I rather like a good sousing once in a while. Look out!'

A flash of lightning shimmered across the northern sky,

and the mare reared and plunged frantically for a second or two.

Barbara clinched her hands in her effort to resist the impulse to take the reins from Bransby's incapable-looking little fingers ; but he managed somehow to pull things together, and they went on again.

' If we can only make the first gate before it gets quite dark, we'll be all right,' she said, in her cheery voice, which was such a contrast to his agitated, wrinkled little face.

' Ah, yes, yes, so we will ! That is the gate now, isn't it ? And open, too?'

The darkness had closed down as suddenly as a black cloth thrown over a cage. They could not see an inch in front of them, until a flicker of lightning showed the gateway and its tall posts. The gate was open.

' I suppose you know the way better than I do,' she ventured to suggest, as he drove through, scraping the off-wheel as he did so ; ' but I'm going to remind you that, about twenty yards from here there's a rather bad ditch, so keep well to the right. Hullo, though !—where are you going? Aren't you driving up a bank? I'm sure you are. This isn't the road.'

Another flare of lightning showed her the scared oblong of Bransby's face and his hands tugging unskilfully at the bewildered mare's mouth. They were halfway up a steep bank to the right. Again they drove on a little way in some order, but Barbara had now gathered herself together alert, ready to spring when the final fiasco came, as she felt it must. True to the courtesy of the craft, she had not once laid her hands on Bransby's fingers.

Another flash of rose-white glare, another wild plunging to right and left. Again the lightning. She saw the mare's glistening back for an instant, as she reared desperately, then found herself all of a sudden sprawled out upon the warm, palpitating body of the fallen brute.

She got at once to her feet, felt for the horse's head, and, grasping the bit, shouted to Bransby. He answered frantically:

'Yes. I'm not hurt. I'm coming. Are you safe, Mrs. Dering? Thank God! Where's the mare? She's run away, I suppose?'

' No, she hasn't,' Barbara called back. ' Don't come any nearer yet—she might strike you in scrambling up. So, my pet ! So, my beauty ! There you are !'

She patted and soothed the mare, who was once more on her legs, trembling and snorting with fright. The rain now fell in torrents, and the thunder was dying away towards the south-east.

' Thank you a thousand, thousand times, Mrs. Dering!' gasped forth Bransby, limping up. ' How very brave of you to stand by the mare ! Are you sure you're all right? I've hurt my knee somehow. Nothing of any consequence, but it's rather hard for me to walk. Ugh !' he ended, with a wheezing sound, squeezed from him by pain.

The hissing darkness surrounded them for miles, and they could only guess their whereabouts by the now infrequent glimpses of the lightning.

## XXXI

BARBARA could not help laughing at their absolute help-lessness. The rippling, human, healthy sound rang out through the streaming night, and at once Bransby felt his nerves steadied and his heart cheered in spite of himself. He was conscious, with a strange little pang, that his ideal woman would be sadly out of place in this situation, and that Eunice's trailing skirt and long trousers would be absolute disadvantages where the scorned russet boots and short habit were now shown to be so sensible.

'If your knee is hurt, Mr. Bransby,' she said, when she had conquered her desire for mirth, 'why don't you get into the trap? I can guess the way pretty well, and I'll lead the mare until we're in the road.'

'Impossible!' whistled Bransby, who was now clinching his under lip with his teeth. 'I could not think of allowing you to do such a thing.'

'But if you faint it will be ten times harder for me,' said Barbara practically; 'and I can tell by your voice that you are suffering a great deal. Do let me help you into the waggon.'

'No, no!' moaned Bransby.

They went on slowly for a few yards.

'Mr. Bransby!' called Barbara suddenly.

'Yes,' he whispered back in faint tones.

There was now a watery glimmer as of coming moonlight. Objects could be seen in blurry masses. She ventured to leave the mare's head and run to Bransby.

'What is it? Are you worse?' she asked.

'I do not know. I feel very giddy,' he replied.

'How is your knee hurt?' she then demanded. 'Is it sprained or cut?'

'Cut, I think.'

'Good heavens, man! you may be bleeding to death! It may be an artery!'

Her voice was anxious for the first time, and, kneeling

down, she peremptorily rolled up his trouser and felt his knee. A jet of soft, warm fluid at once shot through her fingers, splashing her cheek and breast. She said nothing to Bransby, but, taking off one of her elastic garters, and feeling for the silver skewer which fastened her braids in place, began deftly to arrange a tourniquet above the knee-cap. Bransby was by this time so faint that he leaned heavily against the back of the buckboard without offering any remonstrance.

'I must hurt you a little, Mr. Bransby,' she said presently, as her strong hands continued to twist the improvised ligature, ' and when I have this as tight as I can make it, you must help me by trying to hold it in place, and then get into the cart. I'm afraid you've hurt yourself very badly.'

' Yes,' said Bransby, in a queer, far-away voice, and then all at once he doubled up in a heap against her shoulder.

For the first time Barbara felt desperate. The mare was only standing still from shere bewilderment, and might tear off at any moment, dashing the buckboard to pieces, and scaring poor Eunice terribly. Then she would be left alone, for an indefinite length of time, in this glimmering darkness, with her arch-enemy swooning on her shoulder, and only her twisted garter between him and death. Again she felt an almost ungovernable laughter welling within her, but shut her lips firmly and refused to give way to the inappropriate desire. Then she thought of hallooing for help, but was afraid to do this on account of the mare.

' She—she stands very well,' murmured Bransby, coming partially to his senses. ' Where am I ? What's the matter ?'

' Lie still ! Lie still !' said Barbara irritably. ' You've cut an artery, I'm afraid, and it's all I can do to keep this tourniquet tight enough. Please lie still. I'm very strong ; I don't feel your weight at all.'

Bransby was too faint and dazed to resist, and let his head drop back upon one of the broad shoulders which he had so often sneered at as ' unfeminine.' Barbara was suddenly aware of a crisp, curt sound, and knew that the mare was cropping the wet clover.

' Thank God !' she could not help exclaiming.

' For what ?' said poor Bransby.

' Why, the mare is grazing. I couldn't leave you, and
I was afraid that she would bolt and frighten Eunice.
How do you feel now ?'

'Dizzy,' said Bransby, trying to lift his head. ' Very
dizzy,' he gulped, letting it fall back again.

' Do you happen to have a flask of brandy about you ?'
asked Barbara.

' I—I—have not touched a drop of liquor for fifteen
years. I would not touch it now, though I were dying.'

' The devil you wouldn't !' said Barbara, with stern
unconsciousness of her strong language. ' If I had some
brandy here, we should soon see whether you'd take it
or not.'

She gave him a slight shake in her vexation.

' Mrs. Dering ! — Mrs. Dering !' murmured poor
Bransby, ' you—you—you have saved my life. I thank
you. But—but—such expressions ! Eunice—you are
her friend. It—it is terrible—to hear a woman use
such—such——' His head dropped, and he fainted
again. Then Barbara gave way and laughed heartily,
though somewhat drearily.

' To think of my using such masculine language to

such a lady-like little man!' she said at last. 'Why, I actually said "the devil" to him! I doubt if he ever speaks to me again!' And a rhyme that she had once read, in some magazine, began to run in her head :

> ' And I own I fairly revel
> In the way that you say "devil,"
> Jeannie Welsh Carlyle.'

All at once she saw a small, blurred gleam moving uncertainly in the murky distance, then another and another. Her heart gave a relieved jump. She knew that these will-o'-the-wispish lights were the lanterns of those whom Eunice had sent out to look for Bransby. When the men had lifted him into the buckboard, and she sat beside him still grasping the tourniquet, she realized for the first time, with a horrified shiver, that he might have died out there against her shoulder.

It was not until the doctor had come and gone and Bransby was safe in bed that she dared laugh again. And this she did, until Eunice declared her hysterical, and brought her a foaming milk-punch which she had shaken with her own hands.

The next day Barbara had one of her severe headaches, and her head was found to have been badly bruised, in spite of her thick hair. Eunice insisted on keeping her with her, for a week at least, and Fair was sent for and comfortably established in a sunny room next to the children's nursery. The week lengthened into a fortnight, and the fortnight into a month, and still Barbara remained.

It was the last of May before Bransby, whose wound had been followed by a fever, was allowed to come down and lie upon a sofa in the library, although he had moved, from room to room, upstairs. Barbara, who was sitting there when he was brought in, offered to read to him. Bransby accepted this offer before Mrs. Crosdill's dark figure unsheathed itself from the long white muslin curtains at one of the windows.

'*I* have been looking forward to the pleasure of reading to you, Godfrey, for many weeks,' she said.

Bransby looked appealingly from one woman to the other, and Barbara said at once, with her ready good-humour :

'Why, of course, Mrs. Crosdill. I should never have offered had I known that you were in the room.

But can't I find a book for you? What shall it be—a novel?'

' Yes ; a novel, please,' murmured Bransby.

'A *standard* romance, Mrs. Dering,' added his sister.

' Well,' announced Barbara, from her perch on the step-ladder, 'here is a beautiful edition of Thackeray. It makes one long to read him. Really, I can't see what more you could ask than " Henry Esmond," illustrated by George du Maurier.'

' Yes; let it be " Henry Esmond." I haven't read that since I was a boy.'

'Ah, yes,' echoed Mrs. Crosdill, ' that is the book in which that lovely scene occurs where those verses from the Psalms are quoted. Pray let me have that, Mrs. Dering. And how charmingly it is illustrated ! This young girl coming downstairs—she is like that portrait of Marianne Bransby by Reynolds, is she not Godfrey? And here is a—— My *dear* Godfrey !' she exclaimed, closing the heavy volume with a clack, ' is it possible that Thackeray wrote of such—such in-decencies !'

'What indecencies? What indecencies, Lydia?' asked Bransby nervously.

'Why, there is, in this book'—she dropped it suddenly on a table near by as though contaminated—'there is in *that* book an illustration, actually an illustration—I am almost ashamed to utter the words—but a drawing of a man—kissing—a—woman's—foot.' The last word was spoken in an almost inaudible whisper. 'And people have Thackeray's works in their household library!—free to their children! Why, Winifred may have looked at that very picture—your innocent child, Godfrey!'

'What picture?' demanded Winifred, appearing suddenly as though by magic, with a large silver mug of milk clasped to her soiled pinafore, and a large slice of brown bread and honey in the other hand. 'That be-yeutiful picture where Mr. Esmond kisses Miss Beatrix's foot? Of course I've seen it, an' it's lovely. An' don't you say horrid things about it, Aunt Lydia, because you jes' dote on bishops, an' people used to kiss *their* feet.'

Barbara, who had been sitting on the top of the

step-ladder during this scene, her brows lifted and her hands clasped about her knees, nodded sly encouragement to Winifred, during that young lady's fiery speech.

' An'—an',' continued Win, waxing bolder and bolder, ' it ain't horrid at all, 'cause I've seen Barbara's husban' kiss *her* foot, and it looked so pretty that I've played it with Mr. and Mrs. Bridegroom, in my doll's house, so there !'

Barbara was in convulsions of silent mirth, Bransby staring helplessly, and Mrs. Crosdill literally stupefied with conflicting emotions. Then she said, in a low venomous voice to her brother :

' This comes from allowing your wife to choose her own companions against your wishes !' After which gracious speech she left the room.

' Father,' said Winifred, her voice tremulous with passion, ' I think Aunt Lydia's a wicked woman to say such things at Barbara. An' after Barbara saved your life, too ! An' I b'leeve it's all because you couldn't *make* anybody kiss *her* higious ole feet. An'——'

' Hush !' cried Bransby, with such explosive force

that Win's red mouth shut like a trap, and she turned and walked solemnly back into the dining-room, to finish her lunch.

' Well, Mr. Bransby,' said Barbara demurely, ' shall I read " Henry Esmond " to you, or is its immorality really too great ?'

' My sister has—er—very strong feelings about such things,' he answered nervously.

' Does she really think it wrong for Esmond to have kissed Beatrix's foot ?'

' Er—er—I fancy it is more a question of—er—of refinement.'

' But a pretty foot is considered a sign of refinement, is it not? Surely such an act is only a chivalrous homage. What possible immorality could there have been in Esmond's touching his lips to Beatrix's instep ?'

' I—er—these things are, of course, a matter of taste. I myself do not see any exact *immorality* in it, but—er——'

' Oh, well! I suppose it depends upon the foot and the man,' said Barbara, laughing. ' Beatrix had a pretty foot and Esmond a gallant nature. I can't imagine Calvin's kissing his sweetheart's foot, for example, or Coriolanus, or Jack Cade, or Orson, or—or —Bishop Cammersell, for that matter !'

' My dear Mrs. Dering !'

' Why do you exclaim so ?' asked Barbara malevolently. ' Is there anything in the Thirty-nine Articles against a bishop's kissing his sweetheart's foot ?'

' No, no ; of course not ! Only these things have a shockiug sound to an orthodox Christian's ears. I am sure you mean no harm, but I fear that you are very, very unorthodox.'

' I am,' said Barbara briefly.

' I have even heard that you are an infidel.'

' No ; that I deny,' she said, with sudden sternness.

' Then, would you mind telling me your exact views ?' he said, with a kind of anxiety.

' Yes,' she answered, ' I should, for three reasons : first, because I have no fixed, rigid form of belief ; secondly, because my views would be sure to clash with yours, and I do not like religious discussions ; and, thirdly, because I am answerable to God alone for my thoughts and beliefs.'

'I hope that I have not made you angry,' said Bransby.

He was conscious of a curious change in his feelings towards her ever since the night when her presence of mind had saved his life. Merely feminine attributes had not been so solely valuable to him since that time. While he continued to require them in his wife, he had come to the conclusion that, in his neighbour's wife, he did not altogether disapprove of the lack of them, in moderation. His feeling of gratitude had also dulled the edge of his dislike for her. She had even a curious charm for him which was something like that exercised by the wreathings of brightly-coloured serpents behind protecting sheets of glass. Her unconventionalities, and what, to him, were her irreverences, almost her blasphemies, acted like a tonic on his torpid vitality, now made feebler and more languid than ever, by the low fever through which he had just passed. He was like the friend of St. Augustine, who, having allowed himself to look upon the forbidden sight of the circus, continued to gaze at it, with more and more absorbing interest, until finally its fascination overcame him and he could not coerce his unwilling eyes into submission. Bransby, while disapproving of Barbara's ideas and ethics as strongly as ever, had become unwillingly enthralled by her keen personal charm, although this was a fact which he did not admit to himself. He took occasion for stating calmly, in his very long prayers, that he was forcing himself to take an interest in Barbara on his wife's account, since she, Eunice, persisted in having her for a friend.

It was his plain duty, he explained to Providence, to try to soften Mrs. Dering's wild views of life, since she was the chosen and intimate companion of the woman he had promised to cherish. He ended by asking Providence to bless his poor endeavours and to enable him to conquer his dislike for the object of his prayers.

He was somewhat astonished, in the present instance, to find how anxiously he waited to hear that he had not made her angry, and how relieved he was when she assured him that he had not done so. At the same time he was aware, with a fantastic incongruity, that he had ceased objecting to the faint dusting of freckles which made her pale skin bloomy. When this change

had taken place he could not precisely remember, and
it was certainly not in answer to prayer.    He made a
sudden restless movement, and she stopped her favourite
trick of gazing out of window and came towards
him.

'You look uncomfortable.   I will beat up your pillows
for you,' she said kindly.

As she bent over him Bransby caught the sea-like perfume of her hair, and, glancing up, saw that there were
little flecks of gold in the brown of her grave eyes.    He
caught his breath suddenly.

'Are you in pain?' she asked, arranging the last pillow.
'Shall I call Eunice to loosen the bandages?'

'No, no!' he said hastily.   'I would be very grateful
if you would read to me.   Anything you choose.   Take a
book at random.'

He closed his eyes listlessly, but could still see, as
though they had been open, the wreath of her bright
hair, the soft flow of her silkish, gray-blue gown, and the
stir of a dark rosebud which she had fastened at her
breast.

## XXXII

BARBARA was also beginning to think that she had done Bransby injustice. Seen through the magnifying glass of every-day contact, certain virtues became apparent and certain faults assumed that interesting quality which characterizes most unpleasant things thus closely scrutinized under a powerful lens. Barbara wondered at the consistency with which he pursued his uncomfortable principles.

As soon as he was able, he left the reclining-chair, which he had been obliged to use while an invalid, and remained for hours sitting bolt upright in the most uncomfortable attitude. For recreation he was reading Renan's ' Life of Christ,' on which he had a lock put, that he might turn the key in it when he wished to lay aside his book, thus assuring himself that none of the feminine

portion of his household should be contaminated by even
a glance between such infidel pages. He acknowledged
once to Barbara that the work caused him much more
pain than pleasure, but that he felt it to be his duty to
master all atheistic arguments that he might arm himself
with suitable and logical replies.

As for Barbara, she had grown quite at her ease
with him—even ventured to tease him, and at times
to make sly fun of his ruling theories, when Mrs. Crosdill was not by. He would smile stiffly and anxiously
under her quizzing, with that nervous compression of
the lips that seems to imply a fear of their splitting at
the corners. But when his sister happened to be present,
a comical look of appeal would creep over his pale and
artificial little face, and his eyes would flit nervously
from her to Barbara and then back, after a fashion that
only aggravated his tormentor's demure malevolence.

Mrs. Crosdill's dislike, on the other hand, increased as
her brother's lessened, until she distinctly hated their
guest, and wrote long letters of piously-worded innuendo
to Bishop Cammersell as the only means of relieving her
surcharged spirit.

Without hinting such a thing to Eunice, Barbara had determined in her heart to reform and revitalize Bransby as much as possible, even if to accomplish this end she had to use a series of shocks on her subject's nerves as startling and quite as wholesome as those given by an electric battery.

For instance, she sent for her banjo, on which she thrummed passably, and began to sing old negro and Scotch and Irish melodies and love-songs to the entranced children, tuning the instrument to such a low pitch, in order to suit her low voice, that the slack strings scarcely gave forth more than a drowsy humming. This method had to be resorted to, because Barbara's knowledge of her banjo was limited, and she had not more than four or five sets of chords at her command. What there was of her voice, however, had a certain delicious quality.

At first Bransby contented himself with not interfering. One evening, however, as she was sitting at sunset on the steps of the old stone porch at the back of the house, singing to Lois and Win, while they ate their supper of bread-and-milk, he came up and formally asked her if she knew a certain version of ' Abide with me '

which he particularly admired.   Fortunately, although
her repertoire did not include many hymns, she did happen
to know the very one that he wished to hear, and sang
it to him as soon as she could settle upon the accompani-
ment.

Lois and Win, who were seated opposite each other at
a very small white wooden table, waited decorously
enough until she was through ; but as soon as she stopped
banged loudly with both mugs and spoons and demanded
' Nelly Gray ' and ' Widow Machree.'   Barbara compro-
mised by giving them ' Robin Adair.'

' But how can you ask me to sing,' she broke off
suddenly, ' when there's such a voice as Eunice's in
the house ?   What a revelation she would make of
Robin !   It's too bad she never sings now !   It's a
shame not to have a piano here !   Do send for one, Mr.
Bransby—do ! and make Eunice sing you "Robin Adair."'

He moved and gave his uneasy smile :

' You forget I am really sincere in my doubts about
music.'

' Oh, oh !' said Barbara to herself.  ' His *doubts !*
He used to be quite, quite sure, when I first met him,

that music was an invention of the Evil One.' To him she said, laughing :

' Oh, don't be so consistent ! The only good in making up one's mind is in watching the pleasure one's friends get out of pulling it to pieces. It's exactly the principle on which Lois and Win make gardens. Isn't it, dears? Why, there wouldn't be an atom of fun in raking a bed quite smooth to-day and sowing pounds and pounds of seed in it, unless you meant to hoe it all up to-morrow. Would there, now ? Ah, do get a piano ! A house without a piano is like a letter without a stamp, or a dolly without a squeak. Isn't it, Lolo ?'

' Thert'ny ith,' said Lois, rounding her solemn eyes upon her father, and scrubbing even the tip of her pink tongue on her napkin in order to perform the duty of wiping her button-hole mouth with absolute conscientiousness. Win did not say anything. In fact, she was rather frightened at Barbara's boldness.

The next day, as Bransby was standing by one of the drawing-room windows, looking out over the spring lawn, his sister came up and remained silently near him. They were both watching a little procession which was making its way over the grass to the great elms near the centre of the lawn. Barbara, tall and gay, in a soft, pale pink muslin gown, led the way, her baby over her shoulder, its head, in its little white sun-bonnet, making a daisy-like nodding. After her trotted Win and Lois, also with white sun-bonnets, and last of all came Eunice, rather pale, under her parasol of lilac silk. They saw Barbara toss her banjo and book upon the grass, then throw herself down like a child and roll about, shaking convulsive chuckles from Fair, whom she held overhead in both hands. Eunice, settling herself near by, smiled at the ecstatic little creature, and gave it the round ivory handle of her parasol to clutch.

'What very extraordinary antics Mrs. Dering permits herself!' said Mrs. Crosdill suddenly, in her thin, curdled tones. Bransby started and changed colour.

'I did not know that anyone was in the room,' he said with some nervousness.

'I am very sorry if I startled you, Godfrey. But do look! I beg of you to look! Even with your changed views you must confess that it's rather shocking to see a baby given a banjo for a plaything!'

'My changed views, Lydia? What do you mean? Yes! yes! I see the banjo. I must confess that I should not like Eunice to own one, but we must not make Procrustean beds of our views.'

Mrs. Crosdill looked at him sharply, never having heard of Procrustes, and inclined to suspect that this strange term applied to beds was some of Barbara's unorthodox and dangerous teaching.

'Touch pitch, and one knows what follows,' she said tartly.

'How do you mean "touch pitch," Lydia? Whom do you refer to? "Touch pitch!" It is not a very nice expression—not at all the sort of expression which you generally use.'

This was not calculated to soothe Mrs. Crosdill.

'My dear Godfrey, excuse me if I say that you know very well to what I allude. Did I not actually hear that woman trying to persuade you—*you*—to admit a piano into this house? And did you, or did you not, listen patiently? After all these years spent on disci-

plining Eunice in the matter, too! I shall not be sur-
prised to hear that you allow secular music to be played
and sung under your roof on Sunday next thing! And
do you think that you are doing your duty in letting
your innocent children partake in the gambols of that
hoyden? Do you think her negro-minstrel songs are
calculated to improve them mentally, or to aid you in
your system of education for them? You seem to have
grown blind in the twinkling of an eye, as poor St.
Paul did. I only hope that God, in His mercy, will
see fit to lighten your darkness. Why, the very colour
of the woman's hair is enough to warn you against her!
Such violence! Such boldness! Who ever heard of a
genteel, refined Christian woman with crimson—yes,
*crimson* hair?'

Bransby was intensely vexed, all the more so that
he felt his sister's reproach to be in some measure
merited.

'Excuse me, Lydia, if I call your attention to the fact
that you are being as unreasonable, in holding Mrs. Dering
to account for her hair, as you would be in blaming an
Indian for the colour of his skin.'

' " Skin !"   Such a disagreeable word—" skin !" ' murmured his sister in parenthesis.

' I must say,' he continued—' I must say that you show
a personal feeling against Mrs. Dering which is quite
apart from what you might naturally feel against her
mistaken theories and ideas.'

In reply to this daring speech she drew herself quite
an inch taller and left the room.   After hesitating for
a second, Bransby went to join the group on the sunny
lawn.

He found Barbara trying to prize a katydid from Fair's
tense fingers without doing violence to the large-eyed
insect.   Fair was too deeply interested in baffling her
mother's humane attempt to think of protesting in any
other way until poor katy was finally rescued, upon which
she set up a loud roar, shaping her small mouth to the
exact likeness of a tragic mask, and blotting her eyes from
sight.

' Here, Fair, don't cwy, *don't* cwy !' urged Lois, unable
to endure the sight of such anguish.   ' Here's a cwicket,
a bootiful, bwown cwicket.'

And as Fair stopped short in the midst of a howl, and

stared inquiringly through great tear-blobs, Lois extended her pink fist, against which a young grasshopper was bracing his hinge-like legs in a desperate effort to escape.

It took all of Barbara's witch-like knowledge of child-nature to convince Lois that she was not a cruel mamma and, at the same time, to rouse her pity for the grass-hopper which Fair was so anxious to dismember; but peace reigned at last, and Lois grew absorbed in watching a pretty Alderney heifer that was lying in the shade of a horse-chestnut.

Presently she said, in a lowered voice :

' Barbara, what ith the doing?'

' Ruminating, my dear,' answered Bransby, who had become anxious of late to appear more interested in his children.

' Woominating?' said Lois, her small brow perplexed. 'Woominating? She *lookth* ath if the were eating her-thelf.'

Whereat Bransby, rather disconcerted, joined a faint note of laughter to the merry peal that came from Barbara and Eunice.

After awhile the children began to beg to go to the corn-house, and Eunice offered to take Fair to her room with her, as she said that the glare was beginning to give her a headache. Bransby decided to join the expedition, and the four set off along a pretty path which led through a field of clover.

The corn-house was a weather-grayed, square structure, standing on locust posts near the ice-pond, and through the open slats could be seen the ivory-coloured ears of maize slanting nearly against the roof of one side.

'They look like giants' teeth grinning at us,' observed Win, who printed blood-curdling fairy-stories in pencil on the margins of old magazines, much to Mrs. Crosdill's disgust.

'Oh don't, Win! How horrid!' protested Lois, sidling closer to Barbara.

Bransby here undertook to give Win a lesson in literary composition.

'That isn't what we call a good simile, Winifred, my dear,' he said, speaking very distinctly, 'because there is nothing that could represent the mouths of the giants. It is quite impossible that the side of a building should re- mind you of the mouth of a giant.'

Win skipped along cheerful and unimpressed.

'I wasn't talkin' 'bout mouths; I was talkin' 'bout *teeth*.   They *do* look like teeth, don't they, Barbara?'

'But people never have but two rows of teeth,' objected her father, 'and on every ear of corn there are . at least ten.   You see you are still exaggerating, my daughter.'

'Well, that's the fun of it!' exclaimed Win.   'Besides, Uncle Hezekiah Johnson's got three rows, 'cause I made him open his mouth and let me see—an' it was true!'

'Ith thplendid to play dentitht with 'em,' added Lois gravely.

'To play dentist?' repeated Bransby.

'Yeth; we dig holeth in the gwainth and then fill 'em with the thilver off of bottleth.'

This almost incomprehensible sentence Barbara had to translate to him, whereat he gave way to a puzzled smile and dropped the subject.

Inside of the corn-house was a dusty, sweet-smelling gloom, pierced here and there by rays from the brilliant day without.   The large room was divided off at one end, and in the smaller apartment some sitting hens clucked warningly as they entered. The children fell at once into a game of romps, scrambling up the steep and uncertain bank of corn, and laughing as they slid back upon the floor with each effort.

At first Barbara joined in their fun, but finally grew so warm that she climbed up a ladder which had been placed against one wall and seated herself, with her book in her lap, on a sort of ledge which allowed her feet to rest upon the top of the mound of corn. Bransby followed her and sat down beside her. She had taken off her large straw hat and was fanning herself with it. At each vigorous gust, the tendril-like curls above her forehead lifted themselves on end and gave forth a rich sparkle.

Her cheeks reddened and paled under her quick heartbeats, and her laughing lips were a little parted. Bransby could feel how wan and meagre he must look beside this glowing condensation of life and health. He thought, without reserve, that in her girlish pink gown, and with the noble curve of her head bare, she was the most beautiful human being that he had ever seen. That magnetism which for some time past he had begun to feel drew him now so powerfully that, without being conscious of it, he moved a little closer to her along the dusty ledge.

' Isn't it nice here ?' she asked gaily, roused by his movements. ' I dote on a genuine old Virginian corn-house, don't you ?'

Bransby gazed at her almost solemnly, and said in measured tones :

' It may seem strange to you, but I do not think that I was ever in one before, not even as a child.'

' Poor, poor you !' returned Barbara, shaking her head. ' Didn't you think it was *right* to enter a corn-house ?' she then added, with some mischief.

Bransby flushed.

' I am convinced that you do not credit me with a single natural impulse, Mrs. Dering,' he said stiffly.

' Not that exactly ; but I do think that you cry to most of them as the cockney's wife in " Lear " did to the eels " when she put them i' the paste alive. She rapp'd 'em o' the coxcombs with a stick and cry'd, ' Down, wantons, down !' " '

But Bransby did not smile.

' I consider,' he remarked, ' that we are put into this world to curb our natural inclinations.'

' And I,' returned Barbara, ' that we are meant to develop them in the right direction.'

' Of course I recognise, Mrs. Dering, that our philosophies differ widely ; I am a very orthodox man, while you—pardon me, but indeed I think that you will not deny that you are quite the opposite.'

' Quite,' assented Barbara.

' Now, this—pardon me again—but I cannot consider this exactly feminine.'

' Of course you mean according to your views of what is feminine, Mr. Bransby.'

' Of course ; but my views are the generally accepted views.'

' Oh no !' Barbara could not help exclaiming. ' I don't think that you can quite say that.'

' I should have said, perhaps, that they are the generally accepted views among a certain class of people. I really think, Mrs. Dering, that you are your own worst enemy.'

He looked at her anxiously and somewhat deprecatingly, but she was not in the least vexed. She rolled up the flimsy hat and made a little cushion of it to lean her head back upon.

' I suppose you mean that my views and habits shock some people.'

' Well—er—yes,' he admitted nervously.

' But suppose that they don't shock the people for whose opinions I really care ?'

' Ah, but sometimes I fear they do ! Now, Bishop Cammersell, for instance——'

' What would you think of me,' here interrupted Barbara, ' if I told you that I really do not care for Bishop Cammersell's good opinion ?'

' I could not believe *that*, Mrs. Dering !'

' Nevertheless, it is quite true. I think that Bishop Cammersell is timid and conventional, and altogether incapable of owning a sturdy original conviction.'

' You pain me very much,' said Bransby in a lowered voice.

' I am sorry,' she replied, ' but I should not care for you to grow to like me better on a false basis.'

'Yes; your complete honesty is a trait that I always admire,' he put in, almost eagerly.

'And as for always curbing our natural inclinations, I cannot think that God endowed us with longings and emotions only that we should make of life one weary war against them.'

Bransby fixed his eyes upon her kindling face, and gave himself up to the fascination of her rich voice.

'I would rather live one year fully, freely, richly, and then die, than spend a long, tedious existence of suppressed vitality. Why, it is the great sermon of nature, preached from morning until night, through all living things, whether trees or birds or human beings themselves, that through feeling, and through feeling alone, we reach the highest spirituality. It is only impassioned natures that are capable of martyrdom. If our Lord had not had the very fire of enthusiasm in His soul, He could not have given His life for others upon the cross. It is the pallid, emotionless lives that bring forth nothing. Without emotion great results can never be accomplished, and sensation is the movement of the soul. The ground must be broken before it can bring forth—mental apathy of all sorts must be disturbed before human beings can produce high results, whether physical or spiritual.'

Bransby continued to gaze at her intently, his eyes gathering a still, absent expression.

She went on :

' I think that, in keeping our impulses always crushed and unexpressed, we act like some mothers, who refuse to let their darling boys go to school, and so instil into them a certain milk of missishness which all the events of after-life can never quite absorb. I think that in being afraid of our passions and emotions, instead of grasping them firmly and kneading them into the right consistency, we are doing ourselves a great wrong, and, so to speak, hiding under napkins such talents as we have.'     ·

Bransby said nothing, and she went on :

' For instance, I was thinking about Eunice's beautiful voice to-day, and lamenting to myself over your dislike of music, and by one of those queer coincidences which so often happen to me, I picked up this little copy of Plato's " Republic," and it opened at the pages

where Socrates talks with Glaucon about the influence
of music. I couldn't help contrasting it with the teaching of the " Kreutzer Sonata " which you so much
admire. As I have the book, if you don't mind, I'll
read you the bit I'm talking of. Here it is :

' " When a man surrenders himself to music and flute-
playing, and suffers his soul to be flooded through the
funnel of his ears with those sweet and soft, plaintive
harmonies of which we just spoke, and spends his whole
life in warbling and delighting himself with song, such
a man, at the outset, tempers whatever portion of the
spirited element he possesses, and makes it useful instead of brittle and useless : if, however, he relaxes not
his devotion, but yields to the enchantment, he then
begins to liquefy and waste away, till the spirit is melted
out of him and the sinews of his soul are extirpated, and
he is made a feeble wielder of the lance."

' There ! Do you see the vital difference between the
two philosophies ? One, Tolstoi's, teaches total absti-
nence, renunciation even of the good in a thing which

may become evil under certain circumstances—the other, that even out of evil good may be expected.'

'Yes, I can see how you look at it,' said Bransby dreamily.

'And it is the same thing about the idea of love. The sun is fire, and so is a flame kindled from unclean matter ; but the flame consumes, while the sun illumines and brings forth all beauty on the earth, which the wise restraint of nature has placed just near enough to the great orb for us to feel its thrilling moderation without being scorched by its excess !'

Her heart, burning with thoughts of Eunice's starved life, urged her vehemently forward.

'When Tolstoi condemns all passionate love between men and women as sensual, surely he does not know in what real love consists. High love, no matter how fiery, never descends into sensuality. It is the great sun blazing in the soul-heaven, and kindling into life all exquisite emotions !'

She stopped, breathless, her eyes glowing, her whole face radiant. All at once she felt that Bransby had his arms about her, that his mouth was just about to touch her own.

With one swift movement of her strong body she flung him from her so violently that, losing his balance, he fell sidewise upon the heap of corn, and slid noisily and ungracefully to the floor beneath, heralded by the delighted shouts and caperings of the two children, who had rushed in from the other room on hearing some- thing fall. Barbara, one blaze of furious indignation, stood to her full height on the ledge above, and, looking down, saw that Eunice was pausing in the open door- way, outlined by the film of her white gown, through which the sun was shining.

She returned Barbara's gaze steadfastly, and a curious pale smile broke the grave shadow of her face. It was a smile that expressed, at the same time, im- measurable disgust and a certain deep relief. For she felt that now it would be in her power to demand, with reason, those alterations in her life which she had so long desired.

## XXXIII

BARBARA had been at Rosemary for two weeks, and the warm fragrance of June now held the spacious mountain air. As yet she had received no further message from Dering, and a feeling of great depression and loneliness had been gathering in her heart.

She sat at the open window of her room to-night, and wrote in the pages of her journal, now listlessly, now with a sudden vehemence. All during her life, although at long intervals, Barbara, like most imaginative women, had been given to expressing her moods in verse, and it was in verse that she was writing now.

At last she laid aside her pen, and, taking her face between her hands, looked down upon the page before her, and moved her head slowly from side to side with an air of sorrowful negation. Large tears followed, falling slowly and with a distinct soft sound upon the open book.

The lines were irregular in metre, and had a wistful cadence, like the broken murmur of leaves in a night wind :

> ' " Dost thou despair, my soul ?
> Looking through Sorrow's glass upon the world,
> Sayest thou all promises are unfulfilled ?"
> Within, within the voice speaks clear and high,
> And melancholy sweet :
> " Wouldst thou believe in perfect human love ?
> Love in that wise—so comes the promise true.
> Hast thou of friendship a divine ideal ?
> Encloak with such vast generosity
> Some life-chilled fellow-creature, and believe.
> Doth gratitude evade thee ?   Ah, poor soul !
> Be grateful that such sorrow thou canst feel,
> Because the world lacks friendship, love, ideals,
> And hath no overflow of gratitude,
> To waste on what it cannot touch or see.
> To loving eyes, the invisible, O soul,
> Holds more of beauty and of very God
> Than to eyes scientific starry space entire !
> The very blindness of aspiring hearts
> More surely draws the unsure, faltering feet
> Towards holy surge of harmonies divine,
> That, in wide circles, hem the distant Throne
> Whereon, forever veiled, sits voiceless Mystery.
> Strive, therefore, in thyself, O mournful soul,
> To realize in all thine own ideals,

So shalt thou know the capability
That throbs unborn in life ;
So shalt thou find all promises fulfilled,
And no more doubt humanity divine." '

Presently she got up and went out into the warm purplish dusk of the night. A rich breeze moved in delicate undulations, heavy with the scent of sun-warmed strawberries, of damask roses, of the intangible perfume of a fringe-tree, which, in the star-pierced gloom, quivered softly, like a sylvan ghost.

Low over the sad outline of the hills the evening star thrilled through the mystic fabric of the night, like the point of a lance of fire. Small white flowers gleamed through the twilight at her feet. From the shadows, on either side, crimson blossoms burned, with a subdued and smouldering splendour. The thicket was full of birds, the air of wings. In the grass was the stir of a subtle and thronging life.

Barbara walked slowly, her hands behind her head, her eyes upon the scintillating points of the stars, which shone fitfully through the frail and tremulous foliage of the old acacia-trees. What dreams had come to her under their airy branches ! What hopes, what yearnings, what aspirations! She drew a deep, unhappy breath, and tried to realize that, after all, the stars were but as the sands of a golden desert reaching into infinity, not, as she used to imagine, worlds whereon lived creatures like herself, to whom, perhaps, came dreamings such as those which haunted her on summer nights of cloud and shine and gently-pausing winds.

'It cannot be that I am only thirty, and that life is over for me,' she said in a low voice, speaking up into the serene vault of air above her. ' I cannot think that it is all over.' Again tears gathered in her eyes and blotted out the stars. She wandered on and on, and came at last to the low gate, over which a white eglantine festooned itself against the far landscape that resembled, in the wan light, a painting by Puvis de Chavannes.

There was the same bland reach of luminous, pale sky, the same simple masses of great woods enveloped in a tinted haze, the same ample sweep of faint-hued fields. One could fancy austere and lovely figures, in robes of mellow, faded blues and pinks and saffrons, reaping the white clover with scythes of light. A mockingbird was filling the leaf-stirred silence with its delicious clamour.

It is on such nights as this that loneliness seems peculiarly dread and unnatural. The whole being cries out for some comprehending soul with which to share such sumptuous loveliness. Barbara lifted her arms and extended them towards the dim horizon-line in that gesture of yearning with which she expressed certain moods. The empty summer air filled her embrace and beat softly against her breast. It seemed to her that no one in all the world could be so lonely, so forsaken, as herself, and then, as she thought that her heart must break for very desolation, she felt herself clasped close, her head bent back, and the pressure of eager lips upon her own.

'Barbara! Barbara! Barbara!' said Dering, releasing her and kneeling to put his arms again around her. 'Will you forgive me, beautiful, good, splendid Barbara? And will you be a little sorry for me? Oh, my wife, my life, how I have missed you! How I have hungered and thirsted for you!—for your unfailing sympathy — your gentle advice — all your noble self, from head to foot, mind, soul, and body! If you could only know — if I could only get words to tell you — I think that you would forgive me, would comfort me, would take me back, my one love!'

Barbara could not speak. She trembled and put her hands upon his thick curls, as he knelt there in the starlight at her feet. At last she felt that he was waiting for her answer, and managed to stammer brokenly :

'I do, I do, dearest ; but I thought—I was afraid— oh, Jock, I was afraid that you did not care—that you would never care any more !'

She felt his arms tighten convulsively, and he hid his face in the folds of her gown some moments before he spoke again. Then he said, whispering :

'Darling, I don't think that you'll know your old Jock. He's a very new person in a great many ways.'

'Not in too many ways, I hope, dear,' she said, with her kindly-beautiful smile. Then, stooping, she kissed his hair. 'A very thin Jock, I'm sorry to see,' she added pityingly. 'Dearest, tell me, have you been ill?'

'Oh, nothing much—nothing serious. I had a slow fever in Japan. Ah, Barbara! one can do a lot of thinking during a slow fever.'

He got to his feet and put his arm about her. Together they leaned and looked out at the meditative beauty of the great meadows. They did not say anything more for a long while. Then Dering spoke, still in that low, controlled tone, as though afraid of waking some sleeping danger :

'We must begin all over again, darling, if you will bear with me and forgive me. I think that I have conquered that ugly self of mine. I dare not say that I have, but indeed, indeed, I think I have. And you will help me to struggle with it, in case it ever should come back.'

'And you,' said Barbara, her voice thick with tears— 'you will be patient with my faults—you will help me— you will forgive me, too ?'

'Yes, yes, my darling. I know that you are too great, too wise, too absolutely free from vanity, to want me to tell you that you have no faults; but, oh! Barbara, compared to mine they are such little, little faults, I feel that if——'

She turned and closed his lips with a shy kiss.

'You shall not abuse my husband to me,' she whispered.

Pierced to the heart with her beauty and sweetness, he held her against him for some moments in silence.

'And I have many plans for work in the world outside, dearest,' he said after awhile. 'I want to knock out some evil before I am stowed away under the sod. You will be glad to hear this, and about women especially —about factory-girls. I want to build club-houses for them in the large towns, where they can find rest and recreation.'

'Oh, Jock, you warm my very soul!' she cried. 'How life has changed for me in the last ten minutes! I thought that I was to be alone all the rest of my life.'

'And how it has changed for me!' he echoed. 'I knew how generous you were. I felt that you would forgive at last, but indeed, indeed, darling, I never hoped that

you would take me to your heart at once like this.
And are *you* well, my own?—and the child? Barbara,
what a fiend I was! You are an angel to forgive me so
soon! And the Bransbys, how are they? And that dear
Mrs. Crosdill——'

Barbara began to laugh and shake back her hair.

'Why, Mrs. Crosdill was married last Thursday to
Bishop Cammersell, my dear. I have been thinking
ever since how you would gloat over that! She says
that it is to be a mother to his nine children, but I
fancy that the gentle Bishop will find that he has a wife
as well!'

'Well, yes, rather,' said Dering, with his drawl.
'How the mischief could he put up with her? By gad!
that does beat me.'

'It's like those classic earwigs spoken of so long ago
in the pages of *Punch*. Don't you remember? A little
girl is watching them crawl along a bench, and after
asking her aunt what they are, she says, "Ugh! how
can such horrid things associate with each other?"'

Dering laughed, and then asked how Bransby and
Eunice liked the marriage.

'Oh, *he*, of course, is ecstatic,' rejoined Barbara, with that expressive curl of her lip. ' As for Eunice, it is rather a relief to her, as it will prevent those long visitations which she used to dread so. Dearest Jocko, you will like Eunice more than ever, I am sure. We are closer than ever, and she is growing broader-minded, and more splendid in every way, each day that she lives.'

' What lots of good you have done her, my sweetheart!' said Dering eagerly. ' I think every life that touches yours is made better and higher.'

With hands clasped and cheeks together, they watched the dull, rose-hued edge of the rising moon peer above the violet band of the horizon. In their hearts was that deep stillness which comes with hope that has outlived despair.

THE END.

BILLING AND SONS, PRINTERS, GUILDFORD.

www.ingramcontent.com/pod-product-compliance
Lightning Source LLC
Chambersburg PA
CBHW030536040726
47497CB00008B/2471